I0591843

Begets: Fall of a High School Ronin

by Qui Nguyen

ılıSAMUEL FRENCHılı

FOR PRODUCTION INQUIRIES

UNITED STATES AND CANADA
info@concordtheatricals.com
1-866-979-0447

UNITED KINGDOM AND EUROPE
licensing@concordtheatricals.co.uk
020-7054-7298

Each title is subject to availability from Concord Theatricals Corp., depending upon country of performance. Please be aware that *BEGETS: FALL OF A HIGH SCHOOL RONIN* may not be licensed by Concord Theatricals Corp. in your territory. Professional and amateur producers should contact the nearest Concord Theatricals Corp. office or licensing partner to verify availability.

BEGETS: FALL OF A HIGH SCHOOL RONIN was commissioned and first produced by Waterwell Theatre (Arian Moayed & Tom Ridgely, Artistic Directors; Heather Lanza, Director of Education) in New York City on April 29, 2015 as part of Waterwell's New Works Lab @ PPAS. The performance was directed by Robert Ross Parker, with sets and lights by Nick Francone, costumes by Deanna R Frieman, original music and sound by Shane Rettig, props by Deb Gaouette, and fight direction by Qui Nguyen. The Production Stage Manager was Raffaela Vergata and the Assistant Stage Manager was.Sam Kaufman. The Assistant Director was Dominique Thorne. The cast was as follows:

EMI EDWARDS	Jazmine Stewart
INSIDE GIRL	Tia McDonald
LAURA	Jasmine Bryant
MARY B/TINA	Natalia Valentin
ANDREA ARMSTRONG	Christina Middleton
PATRICK	Logan Bruner
DJ MC	Charles Colon
TREY	Jacob Wade
PRINCIPAL PARKER	Brianna McClure
VP FRANCONE/DAD	Michael Newman
COUNSELOR THERESA/KRYSTY	Arielle Friedman
JILLIE LEE	Isabella Sullivan
CHANTAL/CRYSTAL	Athena Ripka
FRESHMAN	Sam Kaufman
SARAH/ROCKER GIRL/GABBI	Daraja McCullough
THATCHER/MOM	Aminata Fofana
WALTER/BRAD BRADY	Stanley Rodriguez

CHARACTERS

EMI EDWARDS – Geek, badass, Samurai, 17, Female

INSIDE GIRL – Emi's inside voice, 17, Female

LAURA – The girl that gets picked on/The lovable girl Emi saved, 17, Female

MARY – Queen Bee in-training, 17, Female

ANDREA ARMSTRONG – Queen Bee, Shogun of the Royals, 18, Female

PATRICK – Vengeful nerd, 15, Male

DJ MC – Patrick's bully & Andrea boyfriend, 18, Male

TREY – QB1 in-training, 17, Male

PRINCIPAL PARKER – Hipster Principal of EHS, 40s, Either

VP FRANCONE – Non-hipster VP of EHS, 40s, Either

COUNSELOR THERESA – Former cool kid turned teacher, 22, Female

JILLIE LEE – Second year senior, 19, Female

CHANTAL – Patrick's online GF, 18, Female

SHELDON – Goth Henchman, 17, Male

DUSTIN – Goth Henchman, 17, Male

THATCHER – Drama Queen/Shogun of the Burnouts, 18, Female

SARAH – Shogun of the Teen Tea Partiers, 18, Female

MOM – Emi's self-centered Mom, 40s, Female

DAD – Emi's absentee Dad, 40s, Male

CRYSTAL – Co-Shogun of the Band Nerds, 18, Female

KRYSTY – Co-Shogun of the Band Nerds, 18, Female

ROCKER GIRL – Anxious girl in the park, 25 Female

WALTER – The real person behind Chantal, 16, Male

Recommended Multi-Cast Breakdown for 5F/3M

1. **EMI EDWARDS**

2. **INSIDE GIRL**

3. **MARY/COUNSELOR THERESA**

4. **ANDREA ARMSTRONG/THATCHER/SARAH/ROCKER GIRL/KRYSTY**

5. **JILLIE/LAURA/CHANTAL/LAURA/MOM/CRYSTAL**

6. **PATRICK**

7. **DJ MC/PRINCIPAL PARKER/SHELDON/WALTER**

8. **TREY/VP FRANCONE/DUSTIN/DAD**

SETTING

Visually, it's an All-American High school meets Japanese Manga.

TIME

The Present.

AUTHOR'S NOTES

Begets is equal parts All-American coming-of-age story and equal parts classic Samurai/Kung Fu tale. It's about a warrior taking on all the evil Shoguns of her land...it's just that this warrior is a geeky high school girl and her land is her evil high school campus. The fun of it is it's clearly a "Scott Pilgrim" for the stage with all the irreverent turns and video game callbacks. But at its heart, it's about bullying and love. My advice is to have fun with it. It's meant to be messy. It's meant to break some rules. It's meant to make surprise people. Now go kick some butt.

NOTE ON STAGING

Because of the short scenes and the constant bouncing around in time and place, *Begets* is conceived to have "seamless transitions" so when a scene ends, actors simply come onto stage immediately to begin the next without stopping to reset the stage. Avoid "Blackouts" as much as possible.

PROLOGUE

(In the darkness, a badass drum beat [Something like the "Broken Mirrors" track from the Enter the Dragon *soundtrack].*)*

(Slowly, a spotlight up on **EMI EDWARDS***, a geekster girl.)*

(There's blood on her fists and lips.)

(From the shadows, her "Inside voice" speaks to the audience.)

INSIDE GIRL. They will fear us.

They will respect us.

They will cower.

> *(Lights up on* **LAURA***.)*
>
> *(Equally geeky, equally bloody, equally pissed off.)*

But to get there, we will have to become as cold-blooded and single-minded as those who terrorized us.

> *(***EMI*** and* **LAURA** *face each other.)*

For us to win, we will fight.

> *(The drums begin to become more rapid and violent in tempo.)*
>
> *(***LAURA*** slugs* **EMI** *in the face.)*

---

*A license to produce *Begets* does not include a performance license for "Broken Mirrors" The publisher and author suggest that the licensee contact ASCAP or BMI to ascertain the rights holder to acquire permission for performance of this song. If permission is unattainable, the licensee should create an original composition in a similar style. For further information, please see music use note on page 3.

(**EMI** *hits the ground hard.*)

(**LAURA** *pounces and begins laying in kicks and punches onto* **EMI***'s torso and face.*)

(**EMI** *tries to fight back, but it's futile.*)

(*Lights come up on the rest of the school who are all cheering for* **LAURA***.*)

(**LAURA** *picks up the beaten* **EMI** *who smiles back a bloody smile.*)

What they don't know is we have them exactly where we want them.

(**LAURA** *shoves* **EMI** *to the ground and punches her some more as the crowd envelops them.*)

This is the not the story of how the geeky little girl wins.

It's the story of how that girl falls.

(*The crowd disperses to find a bloodied and beaten* **EMI** *cowering on the ground.*)

This is the story of a Samurai.

(*Projection: Begets: Fall of a High School Ronin.*)

ACT I

Scene One

(Projection: Chapter One: Playing the Hits.)

*(Spotlight on **EMI**'s inner conscious, **INSIDE GIRL**. **INSIDE GIRL** dresses exactly like **EMI**, however she may not look like **EMI** at all physically. She may be of a different race. She may be taller. She may be thinner. It doesn't matter. **INSIDE GIRL** is simply the way **EMI** sees herself. She is all the articulate thoughts **EMI** wishes she could say in life if she weren't so awkward. She's the badassness.)*

INSIDE GIRL. Moshi moshi, my kewl cats and hot hotties, the bloodied beat-up girl you just witnessed getting the crap kicked out of her was me.

I'm her.

Our name is Emi Edwards and contrary to what your optical nerves are communicating to your brain right now, we're a badass.

We've never faced an opponent we can't outwit –

never battled a bully we haven't bested,

be it simple male or the far superior female, there is no adversary we can't annihilate.

However, this wasn't always the case.

Before discovering we had this particular proclivity for laying down fist-bombs, this was us –

(Lights up on **EMI EDWARDS** *sitting alone at a bench eating her lunch as other HS students walk by her.)*

We are the proverbial wallflower – the outcast – the invisible girl that no one saw. Like ever.

(A group of cool kids sit down at the bench. One person actually tries to sit on **EMI** *as if she weren't there.)*

Yep, the bitch actually tried to sit on me. I'm *that* invisible.

(The cool kid fans her away.)

(She leaves.)

Hollywood has this misconception of the high school teen that posits that the average public education kid has Taylor Swift's complexion and Taylor Lautner's abs. That's just not true. I'm a high schooler. This is my face. This is my lack of abs. And where I lack in clear skin and muscle definition, I make up in knowledge.

EMI EDWARDS. Did you know there were originally five members of Destiny's Child?

MARY. What?

EMI EDWARDS. Well, I notice you're listening to Beyonce AKA Sasha Fierce AKA Queen Bey AKA Missus Carter and she was – as you may remember – an original member of the all-girl powerhouse group, Destiny's Child, also featuring Kelly Rolland and Michelle Williams. However though they're best remembered for being a trio, when they originally hit the scene, they were actually five –

MARY. Hey. Em?

EMI EDWARDS. Yeah?

MARY. I. Don't. Care.

EMI EDWARDS. Sorry, I was just –

MARY. GO AWAY, EM! Why are you so lame!?!

EMI EDWARDS. But –

MARY. GOOOOOO!

INSIDE GIRL. That's Mary.

We used to be B to the F to the F.

But that was before she discovered the power of make-up and her own midriff.

TREY. Baby, you have the hottest belly.

MARY. I know.

INSIDE GIRL. Mary is the heir-apparent to the Royals, the most powerful fiefdom here at EHS. That's her boyfriend Trey, the heir-apparent to the jocks, the Royals most loyal lapdogs in their rule over all us public school peasants.

To give you a lay of the land.

EHS, my school, can be broken down into five distinct fiefdoms.

> *(Lights up on EHS. Though it's an American high school, its design is highly inspired by Japanese architecture.)*

> *(As* **INSIDE GIRL** *describes each fiefdom, an actor representing each clan enters holding a Japanese style vertical banner.)*

> *(Note: As* **EMI** *takes out each clan throughout the play, she will rip down and destroy each of these banners.)*

Artist Alley.

The CC.

Bandland.

The Field.

And that big ol' area in the middle, the heart of the school, is the Courtyard.

Each realm is led by its own clan, each clan led by its own Shogun.

Artist Alley belongs to the Burnouts.

The CC is controlled by the Young Conservative Coalition.

The Field is jock territory.

Bandland is self explanatory.

And the Courtyard is ruled by the Royals, the pretty rich kids who have so much control over everyone that they even hold the authority in check thru their own wealthy parents.

The Royals is ruled by Mary's big sis, Shogun Andrea Armstrong.

And Andrea is not someone you should ever cross.

> (**ANDREA** *enters the stage while texting on her phone.*)

> (*A* **GEEK** *walks past her, but suddenly freezes.*)

GEEK. Oh my God, I'm so sorry. I didn't mean to get in your way. Please don't –

> (**ANDREA** *knocks the geek's book out her hands.*)

I deserve that. I totally deserve that. I'm just so happy you didn't –

> (**ANDREA** *shows the* **GEEK** *the phone.*)

How'd you get that picture?

Please don't post that. Please!

> (**ANDREA** *pushes "send."*)

ANDREA. Sorry. Posted.

GEEK. NOOOOOOO!!!!

INSIDE GIRL. Andrea Armstrong is the realness.

She is not to be trifled with.

> (*Focus goes back to* **EMI**.)

This is who I was just one month ago.

This is where I sat.

Every lunch.

Every day.

Alone.

Since my Freshman year till today, this was my personal hell.

That is until two weeks ago when lil Patrick King sat down next to me and set me on a new course that would redefine my destiny here in the land of adolescent angst forever.

> *(As* **EMI** *munches on her sack lunch,* **PATRICK,** *a skinny awkward kid, suddenly sits down next to her.)*

PATRICK. Hello.

Hi.

May I?

You don't know me.

I'm Patrick. I'm a freshman.

I heard what you did for Big Laura.

EMI EDWARDS. Her name's just Laura. Not "Big Laura." Just. Laura.

PATRICK. Right. Of course. My bad. Just Laura. I heard what you did for "Just Laura."

EMI EDWARDS. Are you here to report me?

PATRICK. What? No. Why would I do that?

EMI EDWARDS. Look, I didn't mean to do what I did. It just happened. I don't really want to do a replay.

PATRICK. Well, whatever it was that happened, it was awesome.

I mean everyone here thinks you're awesome.

Present company included.

EMI EDWARDS. What do you want, Freshman?

PATRICK. Well…um…the thing is – I was wondering if you would…oh boy, I've never done anything like this before but –

EMI EDWARDS. Stop.

I'm flattered.

But it's not gonna happen.

PATRICK. It's not?

EMI EDWARDS. I don't date.

PATRICK. Oh.

OH! No. You misunderstand – I'm not asking you out.

I actually have a girlfriend.

She's French. Named Chantal.

She goes to West.

EMI EDWARDS. You're dating a girl from West?

PATRICK. I met her online. She's awesome. Though clearly from a rough background 'cause, ya know, "Death comes from the West." Which is no news to you since those boys you beat up were from Westside Academy… so, no, I'm not here to ask you out.

EMI EDWARDS. If you're not here to hit on me, then why are you here?

PATRICK. I want to hire you.

EMI EDWARDS. For what?

PATRICK. I want to hire you to beat up DJ MC. Do you know him?

INSIDE GIRL. Daniel Joseph McCormick Carpenter. Current boy toy to Shogun Andrea Armstrong, former jock turned burnout ever since he got kicked off the varsity squad for low marks. Since being stripped of his letterman status, he's now best known for the simple fact that his initials spell out –

DJ MC. DJ MC is in the house! What WHAT?

INSIDE GIRL. Clearly, a very complex individual.

EMI EDWARDS. You want me to fight DJ MC?

PATRICK. Not fight. Beat up.

EMI EDWARDS. I preferred it when I thought you were just a creeper.

PATRICK. The way you helped Laura. I could use that kind of help. DJ and me...we don't get along –

(Cut to...)

*(**DJ MC** runs through and shoulder checks **PATRICK** to the ground.)*

DJ MC. Yo, son, sorry, my bad.

PATRICK. That's okay. I'm alright.

DJ MC. Lemme help you up, homie.

PATRICK. That's okay.

DJ MC. Naw, bro, here.

PATRICK. What are you doing?

DJ MC. That's a hand, homeslice.

PATRICK. I know it's a hand.

DJ MC. Take it.

PATRICK. Why?

DJ MC. To help you up onto your feet. I bumped into you, you fell, I thought I'd make it up by assisting you back to an upright position.

PATRICK. ...

DJ MC. Yo man, I know we haven't always been cool, but I'm a changed man.

I've been getting tutored by one of them kids from The CC and he's really shown me the way. So, see, I'm on the straight and narrow tip now, bro. Do unto others and all that. So I'm sorry I shoulder-checked you. Please forgive me.

*(**PATRICK** takes his hand.)*

See! Look at that! Look at us shake hands like we're old friends.

PATRICK. Thanks. I'll see you –

(**PATRICK** *tries to walk away, but* **DJ MC** *is still holding on. He suddenly turns menacing.*)

DJ MC. But I got a question, bro. Why you still holding my hand?

PATRICK. I'm not. You're holding on to mine –

DJ MC. I ain't holding nuthin.

Let go.

PATRICK. I'm trying!

DJ MC. Yo, everybody see this? Patrick won't let go of my hand.

PATRICK. I'm not holding on! You're –

DJ MC. I do one nice thing and look at you. You're coming on to me.

PATRICK. No, I'm not.

DJ MC. Holding on to me like you want me to be your boyfriend or something. Well, I ain't into all that homosexual stuff, you hear me! It's not natural!

(**DJ MC** *strikes* **PATRICK** *in the face.*)

PATRICK. Ow!

DJ MC. Let go of me! Let go! Let! Go!

(**DJ** *keeps striking* **PATRICK** *in the face, all the while holding on to his hand.*)

(*Cut to…*)

EMI EDWARDS. That's messed up.

PATRICK. Yeah. He does that stuff to me on the daily.

So will you help me?

EMI EDWARDS. You should go to Principal Parker.

PATRICK. Narc on them? You know what my life will be like if I did that?

It wouldn't just be DJ after me. It'll be all the Burnouts. Maybe even the Jocks and the Royals after that. They sniff blood and they'll eat me alive.

Remember what happened to Jillie Lee?

She's still here trying to graduate.

I don't think she's shown up for more than a couple of days of classes this entire semester.

I don't want to be Jillie.

EMI EDWARDS. Look, Patrick, it was just one fight. I'm not Batman.

PATRICK. I just need help. Please. I'm tired of telling my parents that I joined a junior roller derby league. I can't even skate.

EMI EDWARDS. …

PATRICK. Sorry I bothered you. I'll leave you alone now.

EMI EDWARDS. Stop. Okay. I'll talk to him. Just talk though. Nothing else.

PATRICK. I'll take it. I'll take whatever I can get.

INSIDE GIRL. Everyone has a talent – a special proclivity towards being exceptional at something. Now whether that's a talent one would want is an entirely different story.

For example, my ex-BFF Mary is a brilliant mathematician.

*(A spotlight on **MARY** doing equations on a chalkboard.)*

She understands numbers the way an emcee understands rhymes. However as genius as she is at blowing up equations, she hates it. Apparently being brainy doesn't really match her current outfit.

*(**MARY** tosses the chalk at the board in disgust.)*

Her real dream is to dance. However, though my girl has the bod, she unfortunately does not have the moves. I mean – sure – she has some rhythm and can step to a beat, but her dancefloor style is oddly trapped to early '90s grapevines, Roger Rabbits, and what I can only surmise as the dance stylings of early-era Paula Abdul.

*(**MARY** dances. It's awful.)*

INSIDE GIRL. For me, I don't know what I wanted to be. I just know out of all the mutant abilities in the multiverse, this was at the bottom of my want list.

But want has nothing to do with talent. And when it comes to talent, beating up baddies is where I'm Baryshnikov.

(Cut to...)

*(***EMI*** and ***PATRICK*** at the back of the high school's "stage door.")*

PATRICK. DJ MC! We're calling you out!

EMI EDWARDS. What are you doing?

PATRICK. I'm calling him out.

EMI EDWARDS. We're not here to duel, dummy. We're just here to talk.

PATRICK. Okay. Talk away.

(The stage doors slam open to badass music as ***DJ MC*** *struts out.)*

DJ MC. What in the double hockey sticks is this?

What do you two nerds want?

EMI EDWARDS. We're just here to talk.

DJ MC. Talk? Well you two ambled into the wrong Alley for just talking.

PATRICK. I'm not scared of you.

EMI EDWARDS. Hold on, no one here wants to fight.

DJ MC. Seriously, you brought some geek chick here to defend you?

PATRICK. She's not some geek chick. This is Emi Edwards.

DJ MC. Who in the hell is –

PATRICK. She's the girl who took out the Westside boys.

DJ MC. Hold up. You're the badass broad who beat up those two busters from Westside?

PATRICK. That's right. That's her.

How do you like me now?

DJ MC. So – what – you think you some superhero now just
"cause you saved some fat chick?

EMI EDWARDS. She's not fat.

DJ MC. She ain't skinny.

EMI EDWARDS. Listen, I just want you to leave Patrick alone,
okay?

DJ MC. You want me to leave Patrick alone? He's the one
who's got the unnatural obsession with me.

PATRICK. That's not true!

EMI EDWARDS. Just leave him alone.

DJ MC. And what if I don't?

(*Staredown.*)

EMI EDWARDS. If you don't, then I'm gonna have to…

INSIDE GIRL. Remember I'm a badass.

EMI EDWARDS. …tell on you.

INSIDE GIRL. Or not.

DJ MC. You'll tell on me? Seriously?

EMI EDWARDS. Stop laughing. Principal Parker will have
you packing.

DJ MC. Yo, Principal Parker is a punk.

That dude drinks kombucha and watches tennis.

He don't scare nobody.

EMI EDWARDS. Fine. Have it your way. Come on, Patrick,
let's see how scary Principal Parker can actually be.

(**EMI** *starts to truck off, but* **DJ** *grabs her by the
shoulder to stop her.*)

DJ MC. Yo, hold up! I ain't done talking to you.

INSIDE GIRL. This is what you call a reflex.

(**EMI** *flips* **DJ** *over her shoulder.*)

DJ MC. What in the hell?

INSIDE GIRL. I didn't mean to do it, but that doesn't mean
it didn't feel good.

DJ MC. You think you cute, huh?

Well, how cute you gonna be when I beat them pigtails off your skull?

(Music pipes.)

*(**DJ** suddenly attacks **EMI**.)*

*(**EMI** instinctively defends herself without actually having to strike him at all. She's a veritable Kung fu master.)*

*(**DJ** fights as hard as he can, but it's futile. She's too fly.)*

*(Looking like he's too winded and giving up, **EMI** disengages and begins to walk away. Seeing his opportunity, he takes a sucker punch on **EMI**.)*

(This angers her and she levels him with a flying spin kick.)

(He lies flattened on the ground.)

EMI EDWARDS. Let me make myself clear. If anyone messes with Patrick again – and I mean ANYONE –

I'm coming back here for you, DJ. And it doesn't matter if it's you or one of your buddies who does it, if Patrick gets picked on, I pick on you. Got me?

INSIDE GIRL. And just like that…my journey into violence begins.

Interlude One

(Projection: Interlude: The Problem With Being Pretty.)

INSIDE GIRL. When Mary and I were eleven, my favorite movie in the world was Joss Whedon's "Serenity." For Mary, it was Disney's "Enchanted." Which meant – with our powers combined – our unanimous favorite flick was –

EMI & MARY. THE PRINCESS BRIDE!

INSIDE GIRL. A classic comedic tale full of adventure, swordplay, and romance – it was the perfect Princess flick that appealed to both me and her.

We of course had our separate favorite parts.

EMI EDWARDS. "My name is Inigo Montoya. You killed my father. Prepare to die!"

MARY. "Inconceivable."

INSIDE GIRL. We were two happy blissful geek girls who spent every weekend afternoon, dressing up in character and watching endless movie marathons. We were inseparable. We did everything together. All our firsts.

EMI EDWARDS. I just learned how to ride a bike.

MARY. I just got my training bra.

EMI EDWARDS. I just learned how to do a jumping spin kick.

MARY. I just learned how to apply eye-liner correctly.

EMI EDWARDS. I just got my brown belt in jiujitsu.

MARY. I just got my period.

EMI EDWARDS. Hold up. Me too.

EMI & MARY. Today!

MARY. Oh my god, we're so on the same cycle!

(They hug in excitement.)

INSIDE GIRL. Without question we were there for each other. Didn't matter what the experiment or impulse, if one was jumping off a bridge, the other followed with the bungee chord.

MARY. Hey. Can I try something?

INSIDE GIRL. It could be anything.

EMI EDWARDS. What?

MARY. Close your eyes.

EMI EDWARDS. "As you wish."

MARY. Good answer.

EMI EDWARDS. Yeah, I love that –

(**MARY** *kisses* **EMI**.)

Whoa. What was that?

MARY. I just wanted to – you know – try it. I've never –

EMI EDWARDS. Me either.

MARY. It doesn't really count though, right? I mean we're both girls.

EMI EDWARDS. Right. It only counts if it's with a boy.

MARY. Totally.

Wanna do it again?

EMI EDWARDS. Totally.

(*They kiss some more.*)

INSIDE GIRL. And this is the way it was…

The way it should have been…

But then we hit high school and Mary's big sister Andrea started to have some strong opinions about what Mary was doing –

ANDREA. There's no way you're going to EHS dressed like that.

MARY. Like what?

ANDREA. Like that. You look like a cartoon lesbian.

MARY. It's a "Friendship is Magic" t'shirt.

ANDREA. More like a "Friendship is Gay" t'shirt.

There's horses on it.

MARY. Ponies.

ANDREA. Whatever.

Look, you're pretty, why do you have to mess it up with all this Comic Con crap on you?

MARY. I like this Comic Con crap.

ANDREA. No, you don't.

MARY. Yes, I do.

ANDREA. Mary, you're my sister. My little baby sister. It's my job to look out for you. And you and I are going to be at the same school next year.

MARY. So it's really about your rep.

ANDREA. No. It's about sisterhood. The Sisters Armstrong.

We're gonna rule that school.

But we can't do that if you insist on wanting to look like a gay-tard.

MARY. Why would anyone want to "rule that school"? That's lame.

ANDREA. 'Cause we're royals. Look at what our parents do. Look at the money we have. Being anything less than awesome is beneath us. That includes cartoon horses.

MARY. I don't care. I do what I want.

ANDREA. Listen, sis, high School's a different world. There's rules there. There's a food chain. And unfortunately, on that food chain, you're a lion and everyone else are gazelles. You can try to hang with a gazelle, act like a gazelles, dress like a gazelle, but eventually you're gonna get hungry and you're gonna eat those stupid gazelles. It's better to hang with your herd.

MARY. Screw you. I don't need your herd.

INSIDE GIRL. Loyalty. Honor.

It's what anyone would want in a bestie.

But that's all easier said than done, 'cause two months into our Freshman year at EHS and we found ourselves at odds.

(*EMI* and **MARY** *are dressed as a giant boombox. Each of them as different speakers.*)

(*Different teens walk by and blatantly laugh at them.*)

DJ MC. Hehe, I told you they were into each other's boxes!

TREY. What are you supposed to be?

EMI EDWARDS. We're an 80's style boombox, clearly!

TREY. More like a tool box.

DJ MC. Yo, hand me a hammer. I need to nail me a dyke!

EMI EDWARDS. Screw you!

DJ MC. If you want, but it has to be in secret. 'Cause, ya know, ya ugly.

TREY. What a pair of lesbos.

(*The boys high five each-other as they leave.*)

EMI EDWARDS. Idiots.

Come on, they're playing our jam in there!

(**EMI** *starts going, but* **MARY** *doesn't budge.*)

Hey.

Mary-Canary, what gives?

Let's go.

MARY. What the hell are we wearing?

EMI EDWARDS. We're a boombox. It's Halloween. It's cool.

MARY. It's stupid.

EMI EDWARDS. Whatever.

When did dressing up like a classic piece of '80s musical technology equal stupid?

MARY. We're dorks.

EMI EDWARDS. Yep!

And proud!

MARY. No. Not proud. We look lame.

EMI EDWARDS. No, we don't. I put a lot of work into this costume.

MARY. No. This isn't happening.

EMI EDWARDS. Hey. What are you doing? The dance is in there.

MARY. No, I'm not going into there dressed like this.

EMI EDWARDS. But we have a choreographed dance number.

You love dancing…you're just not very, um, good at it.

MARY. I'm not going to do it.

EMI EDWARDS. Why?

MARY. 'Cause it's beneath us.

EMI EDWARDS. Since / when?

MARY. Beneath me…

EMI EDWARDS. Mary?

MARY. Do you know how hard this is?

This school's full of assholes.

The way they treat us and each other.

EMI EDWARDS. Hey. I know. I go to this school too.

MARY. And it doesn't bother you?

EMI EDWARDS. No. Screw them. We're awesome. They don't count. They don't get to count.

MARY. But they do. They really do. And we have a lot of time left with them.

EMI EDWARDS. What are you saying?

MARY. I can't do this, Em. I'm sorry.

> (**MARY** *slides out of the costume.*)

I'm going home and changing.

INSIDE GIRL. And just like that…she did.

> (**EMI** *on the phone.*)

EMI EDWARDS. Hey Mary.

It's me. Em.

I downloaded all of BSG. I thought maybe we could dress up like Cylons and watch it together.

Or maybe…

um…

we could do something else.

Go to the mall or put on make-up or whatever.

Just call me. Okay?

I miss you.

> (**ANDREA** *saunters up to the answering machine (perhaps even whistling) after* **EMI** *hangs up.*)
>
> (*And pushes a button.*)

VOICE MAIL. Message erased.

> (**ANDREA** *gives an evil laugh.*)

ANDREA. Okay. Come on, you slut. Let me see you.

MARY. I don't know, Andrea. This is sorta embarrassing.

ANDREA. It's not embarrassing. It's hot. Come on. You're hot. Show it off.

DJ MC. Yo, babe, what are you doing?

ANDREA. I got my stupid little sister some new clothes.

MARY. Who are you talking to out there?

ANDREA. Just DJ.

MARY. What's he doing here?

ANDREA. He's my boyfriend. He came here 'cause he loves me. Ain't that right?

DJ MC. I love you.

ANDREA. Shut up.

He's fine. Just me and him, that's all.

> (**TREY** *enters.*)

TREY. Yo, what's taking you guys so –

DJ MC. Shhhh.

ANDREA. Come out already.

MARY. Okay. No one laugh alright?

> (*To some music,* **MARY** *enters looking crazy hot in that sorta "Gossip Girl" kind of way.*)

TREY. Holy crap.

MARY. Andrea! You said it was just you and DJ.

ANDREA. Shut up. You look great.

TREY. I agree.

MARY. Thanks.

TREY. Um, hi. I'm Trey.

MARY. Hi.

TREY. I'm the QB for the Freshman squad.

MARY. I know who you are, Trey Beck.

TREY. You do?

MARY. I do. Everyone does.

TREY. Cool.

MARY. Cool.

>   (*They stare at each other.*)

INSIDE GIRL. The paradigm had shifted.

Scene Two

(Projection: Chapter Two: Rise of The Samurai.)

(Lights up on **COUNSELOR THERESA** *and* **JILLIE LEE.**)

COUNSELOR THERESA. Jillie, Jillie, Jillie.

I've been looking over your grade sheets and it doesn't look good at all, girlfriend.

INSIDE GIRL. This is Theresa Sebastian. She's the school's guidance counselor.

COUNSELOR THERESA. Can you tell me why you're putting in so little effort?

INSIDE GIRL. And this is the infamous Jillie Lee, second year senior, legendary slacker, former burnout with a penchant for sounding like a film noir detective.

JILLIE LEE. Are you done grilling me, foggy beach?

INSIDE GIRL. Except her real words weren't actually foggy or beach.

To say the least, they don't like each other.

COUNSELOR THERESA. Well, it looks like if you miss even one more day of school, you're headed back to flunky-town.

Again.

My professional recommendations – because I'm a professional here – not a student – would be to stop getting into trouble.

JILLIE LEE. Are we done here?

COUNSELOR THERESA. I'm not kidding.

Listen, this chip on your shoulder, it's holding you back, turning whatever little personality you have into total grumpy cat, and clearly has you dressing like it's Halloween year round. I mean, seriously, did you use a magic marker to put on your eyeliner? You do know that the objective is not to look like a raccoon, right?

(JILLIE *flips off* THERESA.)

Look, I'm not saying this as your former peer, I'm saying this as your guidance counselor. Let it go, girlfriend. Get out of here. Go fulfill your destiny at being an extra on The Walking Dead. But this war you're trying to wage, drop it.

JILLIE LEE. Fog off.

INSIDE GIRL. But she didn't say "Fog."

COUNSELOR THERESA. NEXT!

INSIDE GIRL. Four years ago, when she was still only a sophomore, Jillie went to war with The Royals. In those days, Theresa was still a student here. She was one of those Royals. And now after graduating, she's returned. Like any in the authority, she works for the cool kids and the cool kids clearly don't like Jillie Lee or anyone who reminds them of Jillie Lee.

Which now, I suppose, includes me.

(EMI *sits down in front of* THERESA.)

COUNSELOR THERESA. What's up, Double E? E-Squared. E-Diculous!

Why are you sitting in front of me? College prep? Extracurriculars? Do you need to know about the birds and the bees?

EMI EDWARDS. I got into a fight.

COUNSELOR THERESA. Was it because you're ugly?

EMI EDWARDS. What?

COUNSELOR THERESA. Nothing. I didn't say anything.

EMI EDWARDS. It was with Daniel McCormick.

COUNSELOR THERESA. DJ MC!?! I LOVE HIM!

I mean – I did – when I was a student – but I'm not anymore – now I'm a professional.

So why did you get into a fight with Daniel?

EMI EDWARDS. He was bullying a friend of mine.

COUNSELOR THERESA. Really?

EMI EDWARDS. Yeah. Really.

COUNSELOR THERESA. But there's no such thing as bullying.

EMI EDWARDS. Say what?

COUNSELOR THERESA. Do you watch Fox News?

EMI EDWARDS. No.

COUNSELOR THERESA. You're probably not into politics – I love politics – like when you become an adult like me –

EMI EDWARDS. You're only four years older than me.

COUNSELOR THERESA. Well, a lot changes after you graduate, E-Diddy. For one, you stop wearing crop tops with cartoons on them.

Second, you start dating guys with facial hair.

I know it sounds crazy. One day you're into Bieber – the next you're into Beaver –

EMI EDWARDS. Beaver?

COUNSELOR THERESA. Sorry, that's something else. But that happens in college too.

And third, you get really into politics. Like me. I love politics.

And Fox News – it's this amazing political channel that only tells the truth – they're like "bullies are a myth," there's no such thing, it's a concoction by the liberal media to create a culture of victims.

EMI EDWARDS. DJ was literally punching Patrick anytime they crossed paths.

COUNSELOR THERESA. That is so sad.

DJ must have really been hurting inside –

EMI EDWARDS. What?

COUNSELOR THERESA. And there had to have been something Patrick was doing to elicit such negative emotional reactions from DJ.

EMI EDWARDS. You mean punches to the face? 'Cause those were the reactions he was getting. The only thing Patrick was doing was walking down the hallway.

COUNSELOR THERESA. It must have been Patrick's confidence.

That must have been the trigger.

It clearly made DJ feel inferior.

After all, DJ doesn't have the best marks. Having to cross paths with such an academically gifted peer like Patrick must have really been hard on DJ's psyche.

EMI EDWARDS. Are you serious?

COUNSELOR THERESA. Yes, I take my job very seriously.

EMI EDWARDS. Yeah, well, I seriously knocked him out, thus why I'm here.

COUNSELOR THERESA. As a professional guidance counselor, my professional guidance counsel advice is...well, for one, you should start wearing make-up and maybe shirts that actually fit.

And you're basically an adult, girlfriend, stop wearing pigtails.

Are you trying to be a Japanese cartoon or just a fetish, which one?

EMI EDWARDS. Can I go please?

COUNSELOR THERESA. Well, we have zero tolerance policy here at EHS regarding violence...

EMI EDWARDS. You're expelling me?

COUNSELOR THERESA. Oh, heaven's no, our new Principal doesn't believe negative reinforcement as a disciplinary measure so instead you have to, well, write a poem about your feelings.

EMI EDWARDS. A poem?

COUNSELOR THERESA. It could also be a song.

I know. Weird.

Principal Parker is from some place called "Park Slope."

Fox News had a story about them. It's a very progressive area in Brooklyn, New York aka a place full of nothing but Godless Communist Gay-bags.

EMI EDWARDS. Gay-bags?

COUNSELOR THERESA. I know it sounds ridiculous, but we're supposed to be politically correct here even though gay does not rhyme with bag like AT ALL!

EMI EDWARDS. Okay, I'm gonna go...

COUNSELOR THERESA. Hope I don't see you again, girlfriend, unless it's for good reasons!

(**EMI** *leaves.*)

(*Cut to...*)

INSIDE GIRL. They say violence begets violence.

What they say isn't a lie.

Shortly after laying the smackdown on DJ MC, more Burnouts start coming out the woodwork.

(**JILLIE LEE** *appears behind* **EMI**.)

JILLIE LEE. Hey. You the dummy who took out DJ MC?

INSIDE GIRL. What I should have said was nothing, but instead I said –

EMI EDWARDS. Yep.

JILLIE LEE. Then you and me got words.

INSIDE GIRL. Reflexes. Good for me, bad for those who wanna step.

(*As* **JILLIE** *steps towards* **EMI EDWARDS**, **EMI** *attacks her.*)

(*She hits* **JILLIE**.)

(**JILLIE** *hits her back.*)

EMI EDWARDS. Oh god. My face!

JILLIE LEE. Are you okay?

EMI EDWARDS. I can't believe you –

(**EMI** *sweep kicks her legs out.*)

– fell for that!

(She falls to the ground.)

JILLIE LEE. Stop! I'm not here to throw down.

EMI EDWARDS. Then what do you want?

JILLIE LEE. You know who I am?

EMI EDWARDS. Everyone knows who you are.

JILLIE LEE. Then you know you and me ain't so different.

You're making noise in the worse kinda way. I've been there.

EMI EDWARDS. We're nothing alike. I'm not trying to start any wars.

JILLIE LEE. Then how come The Drama Queen's now gunning for ya?

EMI EDWARDS. The Drama Queen?

INSIDE GIRL. Thatcher Carpenter aka The Drama Queen.

Shogun of Artist Alley.

It's not a large piece of geography, but her crew's not to be messed with.

Powered by kale, yoga, and a hefty side of stage combat, they pack a mean punch.

> *(Spotlight on **THATCHER**. She's holding a bouquet of flowers. **THATCHER** speaks with an affected British accent.)*

THATCHER. Oh my heavens. I just have to say, everyone, I totes heart you all.

Seriously. You guys are too much!

I can't believe you got me flowers on my opening night. That is just so amazeballs!

FRESHMAN. I'm glad you like them, Shogun!

THATCHER. Aw. Are you the one who got these for me?

FRESHMAN. Yes, ma'am. But it's from all of us.

THATCHER. Well, next time...you stupid little prat... someone should tell you when you get a girl flowers – NOT ROSES! Roses are a romantic flower and, unless I'm mistaken, we're not dating.

FRESHMAN. I'm sorry, I won't make that mistake again.

THATCHER. Of course you won't. But as a small reminder to never make that mistake again, I'm sending you to the shop.

FRESHMAN. What? No, please don't. Please!

THATCHER. Get this freshman out of my face. Enjoy building flats, noob. For that's all you'll ever get to do on this stage!

(The **FRESHMAN** *gets dragged off.)*

FRESHMAN. No! No! NOOOOOO!!!!

(Cut to…)

EMI EDWARDS. I got no beef with her. Why is she coming after me?

JILLIE LEE. It's their way, kid.

They like the paradigm being what it is.

A geek like you making their muscle look weak sours that sitch.

It throws dynamite onto that power dynamic.

EMI EDWARDS. So she wants me beat up?

JILLIE LEE. She wants you pacified.

It's the way these Shoguns operate. They roll in big crews, they make examples out of those who don't look like them, and they stomp out anyone who challenges their position as alpha dogs.

EMI EDWARDS. So you're telling me this why? So I can hide? To go apologize?

JILLIE LEE. Hide? Apologize?

Oh hell's no.

EMI EDWARDS. Then what?

JILLIE LEE. I heard what you can do.

You got a gift, kid.

You can pull off what I started.

You can go to war with all the Shoguns.

You could win.

(A bell rings.)

*(Lights up on **PRINCIPAL PARKER** and **VP FRANCONE** addressing the school via intercom. They both awkwardly share the same mic.)*

PRINCIPAL PARKER. Hello, EHS Wildcats, it is I, your humble Principal Bob Parker and Vice Principal...

VP FRANCONE. Arnold Francone.

PRINCIPAL PARKER. With today's daily affirmation.

VP FRANCONE. (I can't believe they hired you over me.)

PRINCIPAL PARKER. You are all beautiful snowflakes. You're unique, you are special, you are a gift. We're not here to teach you, we're here to celebrate you!

VP FRANCONE. (Seriously I gotta read this?)

PRINCIPAL PARKER. (Go ahead.)

VP FRANCONE. Only you can grade you. You are your greatest teacher. We're only here to bear witness to your blossoming. *(Seriously?)*

PRINCIPAL PARKER. Remember, Wildcats, this school is your educational playground. So play, my snowflakes! Play!

VP FRANCONE. You do realize they're all flunking, right?

PRINCIPAL PARKER. Grades are just a state of mind.

VP FRANCONE. No, they're not.

(Cut to...)

*(**PATRICK** at his computer.)*

*(A picture of **CHANTAL** appears on the screen as their dialogue scrolls across the back wall as if they're typing.)*

*(**CHANTAL** speaks in Voiceover.)*

PATRICK. Chantal, R U There?

CHANTAL. Bonjour Patrick! It is so good to see you ;)

PATRICK. I'm so glad I caught you online. I've had a weird couple of days.

CHANTAL. Bad time at the school?

PATRICK. It's getting better. I made friends with an upperclassman. A Junior.

CHANTAL. What is the name of this friend?

PATRICK. Emi.

CHANTAL. A girl!

PATRICK. No. It's short for Emil. He's, um, Latino.

CHANTAL. Good.

Do not make me jealous!

PATRICK. You have nothing to worry about.

You know you're the only girl for me ;)

CHANTAL. And you are my sweet man.

PATRICK. Can I ask you a question?

CHANTAL. Of course.

PATRICK. There's a dance happening here at my school in a few weeks. I was wondering if you'd like to go. My mom's already said she'd drive us.

CHANTAL. My love, you know I cannot.

PATRICK. I know.

I just thought I'd ask.

CHANTAL. I am so sorry. You know my parents forbid me to do such things. If they knew I was even writing to you right now instead of studying or practicing my violin, they'd slay me.

PATRICK. Forget I said anything.

CHANTAL. I'm so sorry, my love. Perhaps you should find someone else.

Someone there in your own world that you can enjoy such things as dances.

This is all very unfair on you.

Sometimes I really hate being from such a strict household

PATRICK. Don't. I like you. I like that you're different from everyone else here.

CHANTAL. You are very kind

PATRICK. I'm happy. You bring me happiness. Having you in my life is amazing, complexities and all.

CHANTAL. You make my heart sing.

PATRICK. You do the same for me.

>   *(Beat.)*

CHANTAL. I have new photo. Would you like to see?

PATRICK. YES! :)

CHANTAL. Here it is!

>   *(Projection: A shot of* **CHANTAL**, *but from afar as she's at a locker. Regardless, it's still a very flattering shot of her.)*

PATRICK. Wow.

I love you Chantal Larue.

CHANTAL. I love you too Patrick King.

>   *(Cut to…)*

EMI EDWARDS. Are you insane?

You want me to go to war against The Drama Queen?

JILLIE LEE. Not just The Drama Queen. All of them. All the Shoguns.

EMI EDWARDS. That's crazy.

JILLIE LEE. You have a gift.

EMI EDWARDS. I can punch people. That's not a gift.

JILLIE LEE. Listen to me, a bird doesn't choose to fly, it has wings so it must fly.

Likewise you don't get to choose to be a fighter, you are a fighter.

EMI EDWARDS. Okay, Yoda, whatever.

JILLIE LEE. You can help everyone here.

Do you not see that?

For every girl who's ever been side-eyed, slut-shamed, or called fat,

for every skinny boy who's been harassed online,

for every awkward kid who's been pushed or shoulder checked or heckled,

you can even the scale for them.

You can end their rule.

No. More. Shoguns.

EMI EDWARDS. I'm not into revenge fantasies.

JILLIE LEE. Then how about justice fantasies?

Look, why'd you help Laura in the first place?

EMI EDWARDS. Because I didn't like seeing her get picked on.

JILLIE LEE. And do you think she's the only one who gets picked on here?

You can stop them. You can stop it all.

EMI EDWARDS. You are straight up crazy –

> *(Explosive sound effects.)*

> *(Two goth boys, **SHELDON** and **DUSTIN**, enter the stage to badass music.)*

SHELDON. Alright, losers, which one of you trespassed onto Artist Alley and beat up DJ MC?

EMI EDWARDS. Who in the hell are you two?

JILLIE LEE. Sheldon Best and Dustin Park. The Goth Slayers.

EMI EDWARDS. Seriously? That's what they call themselves? I think someone here plays a little too much D&D

JILLIE LEE. Back off. We got no beef with you.

SHELDON. Hey, look! It's the dummy who can't pass Algebra II.

DUSTIN. A plus B equals you're going to get your ass kicked.

JILLIE LEE. Emi. Run!

> *(**JILLIE** dashes forward to fight.)*

> *(But the Goth Boys are indeed super badass and beat her down real fast.)*

(**EMI** *steps up.*)

SHELDON. Aw. That was just sad.

DUSTIN. Boo. Hoo.

SHELDON. Sorta like your entire existence. Face it, Jillie, you're a loser.

DUSTIN. Yeah, why do you even bother?

SHELDON. You. Suck.

EMI EDWARDS. Hey!

SHELDON. And what are you going to do?

EMI EDWARDS. I'm going to stop this.

SHELDON. Yeah? How?

(*She saunters up and…*)

EMI EDWARDS. Fire Alarm.

(*Pulls The Fire Alarm.*)

DUSTIN. Lame.

(*The Goth Boys exit.*)

(**EMI** *runs up to* **JILLIE***'s side.*)

EMI EDWARDS. Okay.

They wanna fight, let's fight.

Show me what I need to do.

(*Cut to…*)

(*A montage sequence of* **JILLIE** *training* **EMI** *in martial arts reminiscent to the training sequences in movies like Kill Bill, Blood Sport, and The Karate Kid.*)

(**EMI** *starts off as awkward, but ends up being quicker and faster than her teacher by the end.*)

(*Cut to…*)

(**EMI** *is kneeling as* **JILLIE** *paces behind her.*)

JILLIE LEE. Miyamoto Musashi.

EMI EDWARDS. *Gesundheit?*

JILLIE LEE. I'm not sneezing. I'm saying a name.

> *(Projection: Anime'esque drawing of Miyamoto Musashi are projected to illustrate the following (Resource material: Takehiko Inoue's VAGABOND).)*

Miyamoto Musashi, arguably the greatest Samurai ever to live.

He became that way because he sought out and duelled every great swordsman in Japan until he was the last one standing.

His first fight was against Akyama from the famed Shinto Ryu school. It was here where he discovered his battle took too long, so he pushed himself to become more decisive in his strikes.

His second great battle was against the entire Yoshioka School –

EMI EDWARDS. He fought an entire school?

JILLIE LEE. Much like what you're about to embark on.

Once he defeated them, he was dubbed "Unrivaled Under Heaven."

But that was not his greatest fight, his greatest fight was against master bladesman, Sasaki Kojiro who was known as "The Demon of the Western Provinces."

The Demon was a far more skilled swordsman than Musashi.

They say because The Demon was born deaf, he adapted by having superior vision. He could see his opponent's moves many steps before they would make them.

If it were merely based on swordskill, Musashi stood no chance.

But Musashi still defeated The Demon, not by his ability to fight, but by his cunning.

For instead of battling The Demon on even ground, he insisted on fighting at dawn on a beach, just as the sun was rising.

To ensure he would be able to be in the right position, Musashi arrived to the duel by boat on the western bank with the sun rising behind him.

He did this to blind The Demon.

As The Demon couldn't see, Musashi defeated him by striking him in the skull with an oar.

Musashi wasn't even armed with a blade and yet he took out the greatest swordsman in all of Japan all because of his superior mind.

If you are to win against the five Shogun of EHS, you will have to become as skilled and smart as Musashi.

You'll have to have a plan.

EMI EDWARDS. I have a plan.

JILLIE LEE. You'll have to stay a step ahead.

EMI EDWARDS. I know where I'm going.

JILLIE LEE. And you must stay focused on your mission. What is that mission

EMI EDWARDS. No. More. Shoguns.

(**JILLIE** *smiles.*)

JILLIE LEE. My work here is done.

(*Cut to…*)

(*Projection: Emi versus The Drama Queen.*)

(**EMI** *and* **THATCHER** *are facing off as the* **GOTH BOYS** *stand by.*)

SHELDON. Let me, Shogun.

DUSTIN. No way you're getting all the fun. I want some.

THATCHER. Go!

(*The Goth Boys rush in.*)

*(But with two swift moves, **EMI** takes them both out.)*

THATCHER. Are you bloody serious? Those were my two toughest assassins.

EMI EDWARDS. I didn't come here for them. I came here for you.

I challenge you, Drama Queen, Shogun of Artist Alley, to battle.

*(All eyes transfix on **THATCHER**.)*

THATCHER. Fine. If that's what you want, then so be it. But one thing you should know, Emi Edwards –

*(**THATCHER** dramatically suddenly leaps into the air and strikes **EMI** in the face with a slo-mo flying kick.)*

The Drama Queen didn't become Shogun just because she's pretty.

Though – yes – I'm totally pretty,

the Drama Queen became Shogun of Artist Alley because she's a badass.

EMI EDWARDS. Gulp.

(Badass music pipes in.)

*(**EMI** and **THATCH** rush at each other and start going at it.)*

*(Though its a hard fought battle, **EMI** finally bests **THATCHER** when **THATCHER** gets distracted by checking herself out in a mirror.)*

THATCHER. No, not the face. NOT THE FACE!

*(**EMI** kicks her in the face.)*

EMI EDWARDS. That was fun. Who's next?

Interlude Two

(Projection: Interlude: The Sad Story of Lonely Laura.)

INSIDE GIRL. This is Laura. Some people call her Big Laura.

She's the typical wallflower – she's into horses, vampire novels, and movies starring Anne Hathaway.

Overall, she's the nice girl.

The nicest.

So what befell her is something I wouldn't even wish upon the worst of souls, and yet...

(As **LAURA** *is at her locker,* **DJ MC** *and* **TREY** *talk very loudly next to her so she can hear every word.)*

DJ MC. Yo, dawg, did you see what got posted all over Instagram?

TREY. What, man?

DJ MC. Pictures of some curvy Junior chick – full frontal.

INSIDE GIRL. No one's claiming the hack, but it's common knowledge that if you tick off a Royal, they don't just beat you up in person, they kill you over social media.

That way there's no escape.

Your life both at school and at home is hell.

Whatever sweet Laura did, she clearly crossed Andrea Armstrong in a bad way.

ANDREA. Yo, I don't know anything about these pics.

DJ MC. You always say you don't know.

ANDREA. Plausible deniability, baby.

I. Didn't. Do. It.

But if I did – damn – these shots are pretty deliciously humiliating, don't you agree?

INSIDE GIRL. For the sake of our home viewers, pictures of Laura have been replaced with –

(Projection: Photo of George Dubya Bush.)

DJ MC. Bush!

TREY. Well, some do prefer the natural look.

ANDREA. Yeah, but I don't know anyone who would like that.

DJ MC. Oh man, check this one out!

> *(Projection: Image of George Bush's "Mission Accomplished" photo.)*

TREY. Whoa!

DJ MC. Yo, that's just wrong! Straight up wrong.

ANDREA. Talk about awkward shot, right?

> *(Projection: Image of George Bush staring at Katrina damage from a plane.)*

ALL. Ohhhhh.

DJ MC. I don't know why anyone would think this pic was a good idea.

ANDREA. You're never going to be able to unsee these.

TREY. Poor girl.

> *(Beat. As if they are truly being sympathetic.)*

> *(But then they all bust out laughing.)*

INSIDE GIRL. Like me, Laura's a "geek."

Unlike me, she's no longer invisible.

She's now became the target of any pervy guy or jock who wants to sound cool.

She was their victim.

Luckily, she's way stronger than me.

> *(**LAURA** storms over.)*

LAURA. You three must think you're just so clever.

ANDREA. I don't know what you're talking about.

LAURA. I'm not stupid.

DJ MC. Sounds like someone here is really ashamed for her support of Bush.

LAURA. Kiss my ass.

DJ MC. Hey. As long as you keep it quiet, I'll do more than just kiss it.

ANDREA. You're bad.

DJ MC. Yo, Trey, I'll see you at the game.

See ya later, Bush girl!

(**DJ** *and* **ANDREA** *exit.*)

LAURA. What? Why are you just standing there? I'm not scared of you.

(*Beat.*)

TREY. I'm sorry.

LAURA. You're what?

TREY. I'm sorry.

DJ's an ass. Always has been. Always will be.

LAURA. You're apologizing? To me?

TREY. Yeah.

LAURA. Really?

TREY. Yeah. No one deserves to be treated the way they – er – we've been treating you.

I'm sorry.

LAURA. Is this some kind of prank? Are you just reeling me in to take another potshot at me?

TREY. No.

I'm apologizing.

Legitimately.

Trust me, I think what's happened to you is screwed with a capital F.

LAURA. Really?

TREY. Really.

LAURA. Cool.

TREY. Cool.

LAURA. I'm Laura by the way.

TREY. Trey.

LAURA. I know who you are. You're QB2, the heir apparent, boyfriend to Mary Armstrong.

TREY. Yep, that's me.

LAURA. You're one of the untouchables.

TREY. In more ways than one, I suppose.

LAURA. What?

TREY. Nothing.

LAURA. Well, um, thanks. Ya know, for apologizing. I, um, should go.

TREY. Yeah, me too. Look, I'll try to keep DJ and the guys in check, okay?

I can't promise I can. But I can promise you'll never hear a bad word spoken from me.

And if it makes you feel any better, I know they're embarrassing and all, but...

I think your pictures are pretty hot.

LAURA. You do?

TREY. I'm all about that bass.

(They share a smile and laugh before they leave.)

INSIDE GIRL. As I said, she's mad strong.

Scene 3

(Projection: Chapter Three: Unrivaled Under Heaven.)

INSIDE GIRL. After taking out The Drama Queen, my wallflower invisibility gave way to something else.

As it turns out, The Drama Queen and her crew were pretty unpopular amongst the general populace of EHS. Apparently, Patrick wasn't the only kid who got picked on by those overdramatic dirtbags.

(Spotlight on **EMI** *as she slo-mo walks down a school hallway to music like* **"BATTLE WITHOUT HONOR OR HUMANITY"** *from Kill Bill as kids are flanking her like rabid fans.)*

(She occasionally stops and poses which make her fans go wild!)

(The music abruptly stops and the fans disperse when **EMI** *bumps into* **MARY**.)*

MARY. Hey.

EMI EDWARDS. Hey.

MARY. Looks like you got some new friends.

EMI EDWARDS. Who? Them? They're no one.

MARY. Yeah. I know the feeling.

EMI EDWARDS. Cool.

MARY. Cool.

EMI EDWARDS. …

MARY. …

EMI EDWARDS. So, um, is that like Childish Gambino doodled on your notebook?

MARY. Yeah.

EMI EDWARDS. I don't know if you've ever seen that old NBC sitcom, Community, but along with being a clever hip-hop artist, Childish Gambino is also –

MARY. Donald Glover. I know. I love that show.

EMI EDWARDS. Me too.

MARY. Cool.

EMI EDWARDS. Cool.

>   (*Beat.*)

MARY. Yeah, I gotta go.

EMI EDWARDS. Me too. I have like a redonkulous amount of stuff to do.

MARY. By the way. I'm glad you took out Thatcher. She wouldn't let me audition for "Into the Woods" last year. And you know I how much I like fairy tales.

>   Good job.

>   But stop fighting, okay?

>   I don't want to hear that you got hurt.

EMI EDWARDS. You don't?

MARY. Of course not. Stop fighting. For me.

>   See ya.

>   (*Cut to…*)

INSIDE GIRL. Yo, this next scene takes place in the mall.

>   (*Lights up on* **PATRICK** *walking through the mall with shopping bags.*)

>   (*He spots* **CHANTAL** *who is looking at a dress.*)

>   (*He can't believe what he's seeing and freaks out a little.*)

>   (*He tries to make himself smooth and sneaks up and pokes her on the shoulder.*)

>   (*She turns around and immediately takes a swing at him.*)

PATRICK. Whoa! What are you doing?

CHANTAL. Yo, why you touching me?

PATRICK. Well, I know you?

CHANTAL. But I don't know you.

PATRICK. Of course you do.

Chantal.

It's me.

Patrick!

CHANTAL. How do you know my name?

PATRICK. 'Cause you told me your name?

CHANTAL. Seriously, nerd boy, don't you take another step at me.

PATRICK. Do you not recognize me? I sent you pictures.

CHANTAL. I ain't never seen no pictures of you.

PATRICK. I'm your boyfriend.

CHANTAL. You're my / what?

PATRICK. Or not.

CHANTAL. You think I'm into skinny geek boys who wear sweater vests?

Stay away from me, Urkel!

PATRICK. Okay, maybe you aren't her. Maybe I'm mistaken.

Look, I'm sorry – I'm not some creeper.

CHANTAL. You got a creepy face, you giving me creepy eyeballs.

PATRICK. Look, I just – this sounds crazy but I'm seeing a girl who looks just like you.

I'm not lying. I have pictures.

(**PATRICK** *reaches for his phone and shows her.*)

See?

CHANTAL. Where'd you get these?

PATRICK. She sent them.

CHANTAL. There ain't no she.

That's me.

How'd you get these?

PATRICK. I'm telling you –

CHANTAL. HOW'D YOU GET THESE PICTURES!?!

(CHANTAL slugs PATRICK in the face.)

CHANTAL. You stay the hell away from me.

I see you again, I'll do more than just hit you.

Do you understand?

DO YOU UNDERSTAND ME!?!

(PATRICK nods and starts crying.)

(CHANTAL snags the phone out of his hand.)

Stop taking pictures of me.

(She throws the phone hard on the ground, destroying it.)

(Cut to...)

(MARY and TREY at their lockers.)

TREY. Hey there, hot stuff! Can I get a kiss?

MARY. Really?

TREY. I mean is it really that weird that I want to kiss you?

MARY. No, it's just weird that you always ask.

TREY. So that's a yes?

MARY. Yes it's a yes.

(He kisses her. She's meaning to just give him a peck, he's meaning for a lot more.)

Okay, that's enough of that. Thank you. That was really nice. Thanks.

TREY. Sorry, did I do something wrong?

MARY. I wasn't really looking for a dental exam this morning.

(ANDREA enters.)

ANDREA. Hey there, love birds, I'm not interrupting, am I?

MARY. Nope.

TREY. Not in the least.

ANDREA. Trey, honey, I'm so glad I caught you. I sort of need a little itty bitty favor from you and your crew.

TREY. What's that?

ANDREA. Apparently some geekgurl is stirring up all sorts of noise on the outskirts.

The Drama Queen got de-thoned. It's no big, but I need recon in case this geek starts getting ambitious and wants to pimp our way.

TREY. Who?

ANDREA. Well, her name is...

(**ANDREA** *leans in and whispers it.*)

MARY. You do realize if you whisper, it's just going to make me ask.

What is it?

ANDREA. Nothing that concerns you, little sis.

MARY. Andrea, that's not cool. No secrets. We're sisters.

TREY. Baby, I think Andrea has your best interests in this.

MARY. Hold up, you're siding with her?

TREY. I'm not siding with anyone.

MARY. Okay, yeah, I definitely need to know what's up.

TREY. It's no big deal.

MARY. So it's a huge deal.

TREY. It's – uh...not a huge deal?

ANDREA. You're a moron.

Thank god you're pretty.

TREY. Thanks?

MARY. If you're done insulting him. What's the deal?

Trey?

Andrea?

TREY. I don't know.

MARY. Shut up. Andrea, give me the lowdown or I'm going to –

ANDREA. Stop with the ultimatum.

Your old friend Emily is the one making trouble.

TREY. Andrea wants me to give her the scare.

MARY. Oh yeah?

ANDREA. You heard any chatter about her?

MARY. No.

ANDREA. You sure?

MARY. I'm sure.

ANDREA. Well, if you do, you best give it up. Your "Little Em" just took out The Drama Queen and that was AFTER she put the hurt on two boys from West, DJ, and the Goth Slayers.

MARY. Why would she do that?

ANDREA. Well, that's the thing, isn't it?

I wanna know.

If her beef is only with a bunch of Burnouts, her revenge quest is greenlit good in my book.

But if she's doing this 'cause she means to eyeball our way, that's where we need to nip her ambition butt in the bud, don't you agree?

Mary?

MARY. What? You think I care what happens to her?

ANDREA. You used to be tight.

MARY. I also used to play with Barbie Dolls. I'm not that girl anymore.

ANDREA. Cool.

Trey, do the usual. Just let her know she's free to feed on Art fags all day, but she steps a foot towards the Courtyard, The Royals will have her ass.

TREY. Will do.

ANDREA. You're sure you're all good with this?

TREY. Yes, ma'am.

ANDREA. I'm not talking to you.

I'm talking to my sib.

MARY. Screw you. Screw her. I don't care.

                    (Cut to…)

(Projection: The CC.)

SARAH. Greetings, my fellow Teen Tea Partiers! I come to you with some upsetting news!

INSIDE GIRL. Sarah Gates. Shogun of The Conservative Coalition.

She looks innocent in that homely housewife way, but trust me, she's anything but –

SARAH. Our new Principal Bob Parker is trying to institute all sorts of new big city ideas here at EHS and I, for one, don't like it! Did you know he's trying to take away our soda and candy machines? What's next? Our liberty?

INSIDE GIRL. Where the Burnouts had a couple of quality jerks amongst their artsy ranks, The CC had quantity. It wasn't just their shogun or their enforcers who were bullies, the entirety of their gang were notorious hecklers, name-callers, and fear mongers. They reveled in making anyone who didn't rock their Stepford Wives look feel like utter lame biscuits.

SARAH. Principal Parker, I don't know where you're from, but here in the good old EH of S, we like our soda and our candy and our saturated fats, yessir.

That's not food to us. That's Freedom.

INSIDE GIRL. Though I didn't have any personal beef with Shogun Sarah, I looked forward to get my girlfight on with her.

*(**EMI** saunters up.)*

EMI EDWARDS. Hey Sarah. It's time for someone to knock you off that podium.

SARAH. Oh look, it's more of those liberal elites trying to crash our Tea Party.

Come on now, let's show these pinko commie bastards we don't take too kindly to our freedoms being threatened.

*(Lights up revealing an entire squad of modestly dressed Conservatives surrounding **EMI**.)*

EMI EDWARDS. This should be fun.

SARAH. Attack!

(Music pipes in.)

*(It's a huge mass battle as **EMI** systematically takes out the entire Teen Tea Party Organization. Luckily, **EMI**'s skills protect her from the barrage of Neo-Con bullies.)*

*(She finally faces off with **SARAH**.)*

Oh, you wouldn't hit a lady, wouldja?

*(**EMI** punches her in the face and knocks her out.)*

EMI EDWARDS. No, I wouldn't. But you ain't no lady.

(A slow clap happens from the wings.)

*(It gets **EMI**'s attention.)*

*(**TREY** enters the stage.)*

TREY. Hey! You Emily Edwards?

EMI EDWARDS. What? I got a fan club all the sudden?

TREY. Do you know who I am?

EMI EDWARDS. Yeah, I know who you are.

INSIDE GIRL. Trey Beck.

Mary's boyfriend.

I hate him.

EMI EDWARDS. I came here to dance my beat down boogie on some rednecks.

But if you wanna tango, Trey, I'd be happy to show you how I go round and round.

TREY. I take no joy in this, but Shogun Andrea Armstrong of the Royals issues you a decree.

EMI EDWARDS. And what's that? I shouldn't wear white after labor day?

TREY. By decree of The Courtyard, you are forbidden to –

(CLONK!)

(TREY gets bashed in the head and falls unconscious.)

EMI EDWARDS. I'm forbidden to do what? Well that was rather anti-climatic.

*(Behind him stands **MARY**.)*

MARY. Sup, Nerd.

EMI EDWARDS. Mary?

MARY. Come with me if you want to live.

INSIDE GIRL. I know I shouldn't. I really shouldn't.

But her just standing there. She's like an angel.

Like, I mean, in totally a straight way. Like a straight angel.

Like –

MARY. Are you coming?

EMI & INSIDE GIRL. Absolutely.

(Lights down.)

End of Act I

ACT II

(Projection: The First Fight.)

INSIDE GIRL. I'm a geek.

Thusly my superpower is that I'm able to obsess over things.

It's sort of what "geeking" means – to be able to obsess over something most people would find insignificant.

For me, it's action flicks.

What I didn't realize was that as I was downloading every Shaw Brothers classic or Yuen Woo Ping flick ever produced, I was picking up more than just their horrible plots. I was picking up their skillz.

So when the day finally arrived for me to be in the same sitch that Ronda Rousey, Maggie Q, and Jennifer Lawrence kept finding themselves in on the big screen – I had no problem calling up their supergirl punch powers on the fly.

(To a musical tone…)

(We see **LAURA** *waiting at a bus stop as two bullies, hurt and burnout, enter.)*

(This is all done silently.)

(They start picking on her.)

(She tries to walk away, but they keep blocking her as they make lewd gestures at her.)

I didn't mean to be a hero that day.

I just saw a girl getting picked on and I thought I'd step in.

If I could talk it out, I would have.

But they were the ones who swung first.

> (**INSIDE GIRL** *walks up to the scene.*)

HEY! STOP!

> (*The bullies turn to her and attack.*)

The thing is.

This is how I saw it.

For them, they were fighting as hard as they could.

For me, I saw it all in slow-mo.

> (*In slo-motion, the bullies attack.*)

I could see all their punches coming at me, I saw every block, every hit, every move I needed to make to end it.

They weren't supposed to go down like this. They're West boys. They're tough.

They're not supposed to get beat up...especially against some nerd girl wearing a cartoon shirt.

> (*As she describes the fight, she slowly shows the audience every hit she makes.*)

This is how I saw the fight.

The world however saw it this way –

> (*Time reverts.*)

HEY! STOP!

> (*The two boys attack and we now see the fight in realtime. It's quick, it's decisive,* **INSIDE GIRL** *takes them out.*)

And just like that, it was over.

Even though they were the ones reeling in pain –

And though it would take another five weeks for me to find out –

It was in that moment that I lost.

Scene One

(Projection: Chapter Four: The Weakness of Power.)

INSIDE GIRL. After my big fight taking down the young Conservative Coalition, though the paradigm of EHS hadn't been fully shifted yet, it was starting to move.

Peeps started looking at the world in a whole different light.

(Lights up on **PRINCIPAL PARKER** *and* **VP FRANCONE.**)

PRINCIPAL PARKER. Good morning, my beautiful EHS Wildcats! It is I, Principal Bob Parker and Vice Principal Arnold Francone with some more important announcements!

VP FRANCONE. (We're actually going to address something important, right?)

PRINCIPAL PARKER. It's come to our attention that our great school, as great as it is, is not performing at its highest potential.

VP FRANCONE. (We're talking about their grades, right? 'Cause their grades are awful.)

PRINCIPAL PARKER. This is a very concerning matter for us, the school board, your parents, and – honestly – the entire world at large.

VP FRANCONE. (Right. The sudden spike in school violence. My bad. That's way worse.)

PRINCIPAL PARKER. We're here to talk about...our carbon footprint.

VP FRANCONE. Yo, say what now?

PRINCIPAL PARKER. This is an extremely important matter. It affects your future and the future of our planet.

Remember recycling goes in the blue bins, compost goes into the green, and unrecyclable matter – which I hope is very little – goes into the black bins.

Remember, our goal as a school is to send zero waste to the landfill this year!

And we can do it, people! Yes, we can! I believe in you.

VP FRANCONE. Seriously?

Shouldn't we be talking about their grades?

Or the fights?

Or their grades?

PRINCIPAL PARKER. What, Francone?

VP FRANCONE. Their grades, Parker. Their grades.

PRINCIPAL PARKER. Right.

I almost forgot –

This is secondary, students –

I don't want to stress you out –

Nothing as important as our waste consumption percentage or our school's ban on gluten...

But it's also come to my attention that there's a question about the academic benchmarks we, as a public education institution, are supposed to be reaching –

VP FRANCONE. AKA most of you are FAILING!

PRINCIPAL PARKER. We have tutors, an afterschool homework program, the local community college is offering free college prep classes to help you all study more effectively.

VP FRANCONE. Or – I don't know – maybe open an actual book and read it.

PRINCIPAL PARKER. Which – I have to be honest – all sounds pretty counter-intuitive on embracing a students' natural love for learning.

VP FRANCONE. What?

PRINCIPAL PARKER. So with that thought in mind –

today –

I – as your standing Principal of the school –

am issuing a no grade policy.

You all have straight A's from now on, so don't worry about your grades! Just enjoy learning! LEARN, my beautiful snowflakes, LEARN!

VP FRANCONE. Yeah, I quit.

I just… I quit.

(Cut to…)

(PATRICK *slumped in front of his computer.)*

(CHANTAL *suddenly pops up.)*

CHANTAL. Patrick?

PATRICK. What?

CHANTAL. Patrick, R U There?

PATRICK. (What in the hell?)

CHANTAL. I guess I've missed you once again. I just wanted to tell you again that I love you. I hope you are having a most lovely day!

(PATRICK *starts typing.)*

PATRICK. Who are you?

CHANTAL. Patrick?

PATRICK. WHO ARE YOU?

CHANTAL. It's me. Chantal. Your girlfriend.

PATRICK. No.

Who. Are. You. Really.

CHANTAL. I don't understand. Perhaps my English is not so –

PATRICK. I met you at the mall.

The real you.

You're not that girl, so who are you really?

CHANTAL. …

PATRICK. Chantal?

CHANTAL. …

PATRICK. Chantal!

CHANTAL. You met me?

PATRICK. I did.

So I know whoever it is in those pictures, that's not really you.

What is this? Some sort of game?

Do you even really care about me?

CHANTAL. Of course I do.

PATRICK. Then why –

CHANTAL. Stop.

Meet me at Old City Park tonight at 7.

PATRICK. You want to actually meet now?

CHANTAL. Yes.

Meet me there. I'll be wearing something red.

I'll explain everything.

> *(Cut to…)*

> *(Lights up on* **TREY** *with a bandage around his head, waking up on a bed.)*

TREY. Whoa. Where am I?

> *(**LAURA** enters.)*

LAURA. You're in my bedroom obviously. Thus all the horse posters. (I really should find something else to get obsessed with.)

Anyways I found you.

You were knocked out.

And I thought I'd help you?

You're really heavy by the way.

TREY. Thanks for noticing. Gained ten extra pounds since September.

LAURA. You're happy about gaining weight?

TREY. Hell yeah. I've been working really hard at it.

LAURA. It must be nice being a guy.

TREY. But why is my shirt off?

LAURA. Oh that? I'm kinda pervy. I wanted to stare at your lack of chest hair.

TREY. What?

LAURA. I'm kidding. Your shirt was ripped. I sewed it back together. See?

TREY. Oh. That rip was intentional.

LAURA. It was? Sorry. I can tear it back open if you want.

TREY. No. It's okay. It's really the thought that –

> (LAURA *kisses him.*)

Whoa.

LAURA. Oh God.

TREY. Why'd you –

LAURA. Well. Um. You have lips. And I thought "Hey, I have lips too!"

Maybe they should be touching. I'm sorry if that –

TREY. No. Do it again.

LAURA. Yeah?

TREY. Yes, please.

LAURA. Okay!

> (*They start making out.*)
>
> (*Cut to…*)
>
> (*Lights up on* EMI *riding in the passenger seat of* MARY's *convertible.*)

INSIDE GIRL. So there I am, seated next to my former BFF, our hair flapping in the wind as she speeds down the highway in her parents' classic Mustang convertible.

Her hands gripped tightly to the wheel as I watch her drive.

She looks absolutely glamorous.

After soaking in the moment, reality finally sinks in –

EMI EDWARDS. Hold up. Why are you helping me?

MARY. We're friends, stupid.

EMI EDWARDS. I don't think friends call friends "stupid."

MARY. You're running around picking fights like you're Inigo Montoyo. That's pretty stupid.

EMI EDWARDS. You used to think that was awesome.

MARY. I also used to think Justin Bieber was talented, so I wouldn't put a lot weight into what I used to think.

What are you doing, Em? This isn't you.

EMI EDWARDS. Says the girl who hasn't hung out with me in nearly two years. I don't really think you hold a lot of weight when it comes to what is or isn't me anymore.

MARY. Touche. But the Emi I knew didn't pick fights with Burnouts and Right Wingers.

EMI EDWARDS. The Emi you knew also got ditched at a Halloween dance by her best friend to become… whatever this is.

MARY. A girl with a badass car?

EMI EDWARDS. A girl who won't even make eye-contact with me in the hallways.

(**MARY** *parks the car.*)

MARY. Well… I was mad at you.

EMI EDWARDS. Hold up. You were mad at me?

MARY. Yeah. I was mad at you. Why is that surprising?

EMI EDWARDS. You're the one who ditched me.

MARY. Sure. Look at it that way.

EMI EDWARDS. What other way is there to see it?

MARY. You've always been good at justifying everything, Em. That's the problem with you.

EMI EDWARDS. Justifying? You left me. At Halloween. And then never returned any of my calls.

MARY. You never called me.

EMI EDWARDS. Of course I did. I blew up your voicemail like a frat boy drunk-dialing their ex. What do you mean I didn't call?

(*Beat.*)

EMI & MARY. Andrea.

EMI EDWARDS. What an asshole!

MARY. Doesn't matter. It wasn't my sister that pissed me off. It was you.

EMI EDWARDS. Look, what did I do that was so awful, huh?

MARY. For one, you never acknowledged for a second how I might have felt about looking like a total dorkzilla that night.

EMI EDWARDS. You used to like being a total dorkzilla.

MARY. No, I used to like hanging out with you. 'Cause WE used to plan things out together. WE used to do stuff that WE liked.

But then somewhere it stopped being WE and it turned into only EM and what EM likes.

And EM wouldn't even deign trying out anything that Mary had even a curiosity about.

EMI EDWARDS. Like what? Make-up?

MARY. See. Exactly! That's your problem. You think anything that doesn't fall into your realm of cool doesn't amount to anything remotely interesting.

EMI EDWARDS. Are you really trying to tell me that I'm the one with issues regarding what I think is "cool"?

MARY. I think you have an issue really looking at the people in your life and seeing how they really feel. It wasn't me ditching you, Em. It was me trying to find my own voice outside of your yelling.

EMI EDWARDS. So you're telling me this girl right here is the real you?

Well, the "real you" wears way too much make-up!

MARY. Well maybe that's because…this girl doesn't really know who the real her is just yet.

She's only seventeen. It's allowed.

EMI EDWARDS. Right.

MARY. But whoever she is, she still doesn't like seeing you get attacked so…

EMI EDWARDS. Yeah, so…

MARY. Thus the assist.

EMI EDWARDS. Well, if that's the case then…

I'm sorry.

And thank you.

MARY. Me too, I guess.

So what's your grand plan, Em? You take out all the big bosses and then what? You become the super Shogun of this school? Make everyone bow down to your geeky whims?

EMI EDWARDS. It has to better than what it is right now, right?

MARY. You can't beat us.

EMI EDWARDS. Us?

MARY. Yes. Us.

Andrea's my sister. She's stronger than you. And even if she isn't, you beating her up won't stop her. She didn't become Shogun because of her muscle. She became Shogun because she's scary. Real Scary. She doesn't take people out by hitting them in the face.

She hits them where it really hurts. She's smart. Smarter than you.

I just – I don't want to see you hurt.

EMI EDWARDS. You don't?

MARY. No. Of course not. We might not be besties anymore.

But you're still Em. I'm still Mary-Canary. I care about you.

Please. Just. Think this over. Please.

EMI EDWARDS. "As you wish."

(**EMI** *leans over and kisses* **MARY**.)

MARY. Whoa, what are you doing?

EMI EDWARDS. What are YOU doing?

MARY. You kissed me.

EMI EDWARDS. No. YOU kissed ME.

MARY. No, I didn't –

Hold up.

Emi…

Are you – um – you know –

EMI EDWARDS. What?

I don't know.

I mean I don't like sports or anything,

but I guess…

women's basketball could be cool.

MARY. Oh god.

Look, I'm not –

You know I'm not –

I have a boyfriend.

EMI EDWARDS. You mean the guy you knocked out with a bat?

MARY. Yeah. Okay, maybe he's not "the one," but he loves me. And, well, even if I don't love him, that still doesn't mean that I'm –

EMI EDWARDS. I get it.

I'm sorry.

I overstepped.

It's just – I like talking to you again.

I just got over-excited.

MARY. Clearly.

EMI EDWARDS. Forget that ever happened.

MARY. Cool. Nothing happened. We're cool.

EMI EDWARDS. Cool.

     (They sit quietly there for a moment.)

     (And then suddenly they mutually start making out again.)

(Cut to…)

*(**TREY** and **LAURA** still making out.)*

TREY. I love you.

LAURA. What?

TREY. What? Oh God, why did I say that?

LAURA. Did you just tell me you loved me?

TREY. No.

LAURA. You just told me you love me.

TREY. Mary and I have been together for almost two years. I love her. It's just –

LAURA. Does she not do this with you?

TREY. Do what?

LAURA. This.

TREY. She holds my hand.

In public.

And we kiss…

whenever I ask…

Or when we're on the Homecoming court and there's a photo-op.

LAURA. Wow. That's really romantic.

You should put that in a book –

And sell it –

On Amazon.

TREY. Okay, so we might not have the most steamy of relationships.

LAURA. So this right now is a pretty big deal, huh?

TREY. It's not for you?

LAURA. Believe it or not, I've never had the best self-esteem. So I may rush to this faster than some since, well, I know what to do here even when I don't know what to do out there.

TREY. I don't think any of us actually know what we're doing out there so you're not alone.

LAURA. Good to know.

So you love me?

TREY. Clearly I just got carried away –

LAURA. I'm kidding.

TREY. Look, I'm not really as bad as people think I am.

LAURA. I'm not as good as people think I am.

TREY. Bull.

LAURA. It's true.

TREY. But you're so nice –

LAURA. Just 'cause I'm nice doesn't mean I'm not angry.

Just 'cause I don't stomp around with a grimace on my face and balled up fists doesn't mean I'm not boiling with rage.

Sometimes I really don't like being the "invisible girl" all the time.

Sometimes I would like to be seen.

TREY. I don't like me every day either.

    (Beat.)

Look, Laura, I like you – I do – but –

LAURA. I get it.

Mary makes better arm candy.

TREY. It has nothing to do with arm candy, it's just –

Mary and I have really put a lot of time in with each other,

we share the same circle of friends,

our lives are entangled.

It's messy.

I'm sorry.

LAURA. Yeah. Me too.

    (Cut to…)

    *(**PATRICK** is waiting in the park, super dressed up and holding flowers. He's practicing what to say.)*

PATRICK. Okay, so maybe you don't look like your picture –

That's cool.

So what if you're fat.

Or old.

Like super old.

And super fat.

And not French.

It doesn't matter.

I like you.

I don't share myself like that with anyone.

So I'm okay with –

> (*A dishevelled* **ROCKER GIRL** *wearing a bright red hoodie enters the stage.*)
>
> (*She's visibly nervous and anxious.*)

Oh god.

Okay.

So she looks like Marilyn Manson.

That's cool.

I could totally get into, um, piercings as well.

> (**PATRICK** *approaches.*)

Ahem. Hi. It's so nice to –

ROCKER GIRL. You a cop?

PATRICK. What?

ROCKER GIRL. Look, I'm just minding my own business. I ain't doing nothing.

PATRICK. I'm not a cop.

ROCKER GIRL. Seriously, you can look through my stuff. There's nothing there. I'm clean.

PATRICK. I'm not a cop.

ROCKER GIRL. What?

PATRICK. I'm. Not. A. Cop.

ROCKER GIRL. You're not? Then why in the hell are you talking to me?

PATRICK. What?

ROCKER GIRL. Mind your damn business!

I didn't ask you to come over here!

Ya know what, four-eyes, maybe I should take those flowers you got there and shove them up your ass!

How would you like that?

PATRICK. No. Stay away from me!

> *(She goes to attack him, suddenly* **WALTER** *enters and pulls her off of him. (He has a subtle red bowtie on).)*

WALTER. Hey! Leave him alone! Go away. GO!

ROCKER GIRL. Man, this park used to be nice. Nothing but lowlifes now. Peace!

> *(She leaves.)*

PATRICK. Hey. Thanks.

WALTER. No problem.

PATRICK. Patrick.

WALTER. Walter. It's nice to meet you. Sorry about the weird chick, I should have picked a better meeting spot for us.

PATRICK. What?

WALTER. Yeah, I'm – uh – the person you've been talking to on the computer. Surprise!

PATRICK. You?

WALTER. Yes.

PATRICK. But you're a / dude.

WALTER. I know.

But before you freak, just hear me out.

Listen – I know Chantal – or at least the version of Chantal that you knew – was this complete concoction, but all those conversations we had –

the six months of us talking –

every text, tweet, and chat –

those were real.

That wasn't a fabrication –

It wasn't a prank –

I wasn't catfishing you –

I just – I thought it'd be fun to try on someone else's skin for a moment and then when it attracted you and we started talking and the thing is –

the stuff you go through –

the bullies, your parents, the fact that you've never been kissed –

well, I get that.

I've lived that.

I am that.

I'm you just at a different school

And the thing is when I told you I loved you, I meant it.

I mean it.

I fell in love with you, Patrick King.

And even if you don't feel the same way, I just had to tell you that in person just once.

I love you.

Please say something.

Please.

PATRICK. I didn't care what you were going to look like.

Fat. Super skinny. In a wheel chair. Old. It didn't matter –

WALTER. It doesn't?

PATRICK. But not this.

This is the one thing you couldn't be.

You just had to be a girl. That's all. Just a girl and you were going to have my heart.

Forever.

WALTER. I'm so sorry.

PATRICK. You're sorry? Sorry?

You just killed the reason I look forward to waking up everyday.

You destroyed the one thing that made me feel okay on the daily.

You murdered my Chantal.

You killed my dream.

So, no, screw you and your sorry!

I hate you!

> *(**PATRICK** grabs a rock and smashes it against **WALTER**'s skull.)*

WALTER. OW!

PATRICK. FUCK YOU!

> *(**PATRICK** rears back to hit **WALTER** again –.)*

WALTER. Please don't! Please!

PATRICK. Don't ever try to contact me again.

> *(**PATRICK** drops the rock and exits as **WALTER** holds his head, crying.)*
>
> *(Cut to...)*
>
> *(**ANDREA** on the phone.)*

ANDREA. Hello, is this the parents of Emily Edwards?

Hi. I'm calling from the school.

I know you two don't necessarily do this together. But I felt that you both should know what your daughter Emily has been up to...

INSIDE GIRL. Andrea Armstrong: she finds you where you're weak and hits you there.

Scene Two

(Projection: Chapter Five: History of Violence.)

INSIDE GIRL. These are my parents.

(Lights up on her **MOM***.)*

Corporate suit, corporate job, and left my dad for the least corporate guy EVER.

(Lights up on K-DAWG.)

That's K-Dawg, her boyfriend. He looks like Flea from the Red Hot Chili Peppers if Flea were beaten in the face with heroin and said "dude" alot.

K-DAWG. Duuuude.

INSIDE GIRL. And this is my dad.

(Lights up on an empty spot onstage.)

Wait for it.

(DAD *walks into the spotlight while looking at his phone.)*

There he is.

He's a good looking guy. Or that's what people tell me. When he's around, he awesome –

(DAD *leaves.)*

That is when he's around.

So who took care of me when my parental units were a self-centered mom and absentee dad?

Simple.

The only parent I ever needed.

(Lights up on a TV.)

Netflix.

Hulu.

YouTube.

Spotify.

Pirate Bay.

iTunes.

Google Play.

These are the peeps who cuddle me to sleep.

The folks who make me feel safe at night.

This is who I came home to.

But don't feel sad for me.

Unlike my mom and dad, I can always count on them.

They are always there.

Well, except for shows on FOX that get cancelled way before their prime.

My dad was Admiral Adama and my mom Buffy Summers.

And my backyard was the imagination of Disney, the Marvel Universe, Bad Robot, and Mutant Entertainment.

I was taught how to take on the world solo because…

Well, that's the only way I've ever seen the world.

And I'm just fine.

Really good.

Totally.

I'm super awesome.

But the word "family" feels very odd to me.

>   (**EMI** *walks into her house.*)

>   (*Standing there are both her parents.*)

DAD. Hey there, Emi Bear.

MOM. HEY!

EMI EDWARDS. Um, this is weird.

INSIDE GIRL. My parents. Together. In the same room. To say the least, this never happens.

MOM. We got a call from your school.

DAD. We're worried about you.

EMI EDWARDS. I have straight A's.

DAD. It's not your grades we're worried about.

INSIDE GIRL. My dad staring at me with his big saucer eyes, my mom pacing in the background like a drug addict waiting for their next fix –

EMI EDWARDS. Then what is it?

MOM. What are these?

> (**MOM** *throws a stack of bloody clothes in* **EMI**'s *lap.*)

EMI EDWARDS. Clothes.

MOM. Don't be a smartass!

DAD. Hey! We're not here to yell at you.

MOM. Yes, we are. We definitely are.

DAD. No, we're not.

INSIDE GIRL. These are my parents with their powers combined.

Impressive, right?

It's like a bad cop show where I'm getting interrogated for a crime I didn't commit.

> (*Light shift to make it all look like a cop show interrogation.*)

MOM. Look, Pippi Longstockings, we can do this the easy way or the fun way.

EMI EDWARDS. What's the fun way?

MOM. Me kicking the snot out of you until you spill your guts.

EMI EDWARDS. That doesn't sound fun.

MOM. Maybe not for you.

DAD. What my former partner here is trying to convey – minus the red face and throbbing neck veins – is it'll be easier here on you if you can be straight up with us.

MOM. Straight up, what's with your clothes looking like giant used tampons?

Speak, geek, before we make you talk.

DAD. What are you doing, Emi Bear?

MOM. She's beating up kids clearly.

It's exactly what that counselor person told us.

She's a bully.

EMI EDWARDS. No, I'm not!

DAD. I thought we raised you better than this.

MOM. Are you a psychopath?

DAD. I have to say I'm really disappointed in you.

MOM. Aka YOU SUCK.

DAD. What are we going to do?

INSIDE GIRL. I wasn't always a fighter. But as I've learned, you can only push the girl so hard before she pushes back even harder.

MOM. See! No respect! It's because you don't know how to discipline.

DAD. Maybe if you knew how to talk about anything other than yourself or "K-Dawg," maybe you could help parent too.

MOM. Says the man who's never home.

DAD. Accuses the woman who spends more money on her boyfriend than her kid.

MOM. Screw you!

DAD. Screw you.

EMI EDWARDS & INSIDE GIRL. Screw you both!

DAD. Emi?

EMI EDWARDS. Ya know what? Maybe it's actually both your faults – have you ever thought / about that?

INSIDE GIRL. Maybe if you both didn't have your own heads up your own butts trying to one-up the other, I'd be far more / well-adjusted than I am.

EMI EDWARDS. Maybe if it weren't for your dumb job that always takes you out of town or you constantly wasting your breath on justifying your loser boyfriend to me, maybe I'd feel supported and loved instead of so damn angry / all the time.

INSIDE GIRL. Or maybe it has nothing to do with either of you and everything to do with the crap-ass school I'm at where the self-centered are celebrated and the outsiders are ousted.

EMI EDWARDS & INSIDE GIRL. Maybe!

EMI EDWARDS. But – either way – you sitting here now is a little too little and a lot too late.

EMI EDWARDS & INSIDE GIRL. So screw you both!

INSIDE GIRL. Of course I didn't actually say any of that. Instead I say –

EMI EDWARDS. Stop!

I'm sorry.

It won't happen again.

I promise.

Just don't fight.

DAD. Emi?

EMI EDWARDS. Just stop fighting.

I can't take it.

I really just can't take it.

MOM. I'm so sorry.

DAD. Come here.

(*They hug her.*)

INSIDE GIRL. Aw.

Such a sweet scene of familial love and support.

Too bad it's BS.

'Cause as soon as they're not around –

(*Cut to…*)

EMI EDWARDS. I need something to hit.

Hard.

Real hard.

PATRICK. I'm with you.

MARY. I thought you said you were done.

EMI EDWARDS. That's before someone decided to make it personal.

PATRICK. What's with the cheerleader hanging with us?

I don't trust no cheerleaders.

MARY. No worries, Geek Caveboy, "Cheerleader no trust you either."

PATRICK. Screw you.

MARY. I'm not going to help you do this.

EMI EDWARDS. That's okay, I don't need your help.

MARY. I'm serious. I'm not going to bail you out again.

EMI EDWARDS. That's fine. I'm fine. The only thing that's not going to be fine are the assholes I hit.

PATRICK. Where are we going?

(Projection: Bandland.)

INSIDE GIRL. Bandland. Ruled by the twins, Krysty and Crystal Tillman. They're like the Switzerland of EHS. That is if Switzerland was hugely backstabby and would do anything – and I mean anything – to be in the favor of the most powerful nations in the UN. 'Cause though Bandlanders may look like my fellow peeps, make no mistake, they're not. They're selfhating geeks who'd rather kiss up to the Royals than support their fellow outsiders.

Simply put, though they may not be the ones actively pushing you in front of the bus, they're the ones who stand there and just turn their backs as you're getting run over.

They're way worse.

(Lights up on two bandgeeks who speak with lisps.)

KRYSTY. Oh God, it's Emi Edwards. It's really her! She's here!

CRYSTAL. Hey there, awesome Emi! Welcome to our corner of the world. We are so stoked to see you here!

KRYSTY. Also, we just want to remind you that we have no beef with you. Seriously no beef at all.

CRYSTAL. Like we're totally Vegan.

KRYSTY. So, may I ask, why are you here?

CRYSTAL. Please say to play Twister. We really like Twister.

EMI EDWARDS. I think you know why I'm here.

KRYSTY. But why? We love you here.

CRYSTAL. We're basically the same!

KRYSTY & CRYSTAL. Fellow geeks!

CRYSTAL. High five'sies?

EMI EDWARDS. …

KRYSTY. She does not want to high five.

CRYSTAL. Fist bump?

EMI EDWARDS. We're not friends. You've never talked to me before today, so don't pretend we're cool.

We're not cool.

CRYSTAL. She seems mad.

KRYSTY. She does.

CRYSTAL. What do we do?

KRYSTY. Well, I guess this leaves us no choice really.

CRYSTAL. We're totally in a corner.

KRYSTY. If Bandland is what you want, Emi Edward, then here goes…

(**EMI** *and her crew fall into fight positions.*)

KRYSTY & CRYSTAL. It's yours.

MARY. What?

KRYSTY. We wish no violence done to any of our people.

CRYSTAL. We forfeit our titles of Shogun to you, honorable Emi Edwards of Murmil Heights.

EMI EDWARDS. You're being serious?

KRYSTY & CRYSTAL. Totes.

KRYSTY. But one thing –

EMI EQWDWARDS. What's that?

> (**KRYSTY & CRYSTAL** *pull out a large remote control and push a button!*)

KRYSTY & CRYSTAL. EHS MARCHING BANDBOT GO!

EMI EDWARDS. What? You're sending the marching band out to get me? Like I'm gonna be scared of a bunch of...

> *(CLOMP.)*

> *(CLOMP.)*

> *(CLOMP.)*

> *(A giant robot enter the stage.)*

MARY. What in the hell is that?

KRYSTY. Bandland is full of nerds.

CRYSTAL. Nerds make robots.

KRYSTY. Big robots.

KRYSTY & CRYSTAL. ATTACK BANDBOT FIGHT!!!

> *(The giant robot attacks* **EMI.** *She's no good at defending herself from it. It's beating her down pretty decisively.)*

MARY. Dammit, Em!

EMI EDWARDS. Help me, Mary. Help!

MARY. I really really hate you sometimes.

> (**MARY** *cartwheels into the action and keeps the robot from hurting* **EMI.***)*

> (**EMI** *leaps up beside her.)*

EMI EDWARDS. Just like old times.

MARY. Inconceivable!

EMI EDWARDS. Let's do this!

> *(And with their powers combined, they fight the bandbot.)*

(They almost lose until **MARY** *luckily spots and hits the "power switch" on it, turning the bandbot off.)*

(The girls now turn their attention on **KRYSTY** *and* **CRYSTAL**.*)*

KRYSTY. Ya know what? This time we really do give up.

CRYSTAL. Yeah. Totally.

*(**KRYSTY** and **CRYSTAL** run away.)*

EMI EDWARDS. That. Was.

MARY & EMI. AWESOME!!!!

*(**EMI** and **MARY** hug each other in celebration.)*

PATRICK. That's so hot.

MARY & EMI. Shut up!

*(**MARY** saunters up and rips down the Bandland banner. She hands it to **EMI** and kneels.)*

(Cut to...)

*(**ANDREA** in the gymnasium.)*

ANDREA. WHAT!?!

DJ MC. Yeah. I knew this was gonna make you mad.

ANDREA. Mary is helping Emily Edwards now? My sister!?! MY SISTER!?!

DJ MC. Yep.

ANDREA. That little – AHHHH!

DJ MC. That geek and her crew now control more area of the school than both the Jocks and the Royals combined. What are we gonna do?

ANDREA. Get me a geek. Get me twenty geeks. A hundred. I don't care how many nerds you gotta beat up to do this, but I need someone to hack into her Twitter, her Dropbox, Tumblr, Snapchat, ANYTHING – but I want something that will destroy her. Humiliate her. And I want it now. Do you understand?

DJ MC. Yes, ma'am.

ANDREA. GOOOO!

(TREY enters...)

TREY. Um, Shogun Andrea?

ANDREA. What do you want?

TREY. Just one little thing.

ANDREA. What, fool? What?

(EMI and her crew enter.)

EMI EDWARDS. Bad guys are here.

ANDREA. How'd you –

How'd she get in here so easily?

EMI EDWARDS. Turns out, Andrea, alotta peeps don't like you. They kinda just Red-Sea parted for us all the way here.

TREY. She used a giant band robot to take out the football team.

(Quickly, in the background, we see the Bandbot chasing the Jocks who are running away in fear.)

EMI EDWARDS. Oh yeah. And there was that too.

ANDREA. So you really want to fight me?

EMI EDWARDS. Yeah. Thus the outfit.

These are my fight-y pants. They're stretchy.

ANDREA. Think this through, Emily, what you're doing is wrong. It goes against the natural order of things.

EMI EDWARDS. You're serious? You think you guys running the school and bullying anyone who doesn't look like you is the "natural order of things"? Are you insane?

ANDREA. Listen to me. No one hates bears because they eat fish.

No one calls for the mass extinction of owls because they have to prey on mice.

It's the food chain, Emily – big animals eat small animals. Small animals eat even smaller animals. And those teeny little worthless animals eat bugs.

EMI EDWARDS. And what am I supposed to be in that equation? One of those little worthless animals?

Or a bug.

ANDREA. Neither. You're smaller. A virus that eats away at everything above it.

EMI EDWARDS. Aw. That's sort of a compliment. Thank you!

ANDREA. What you're doing – what you're trying to – isn't some heroic act of vigilante justice.

What you're doing is upsetting the entire food chain.

You're throwing piranhas into the river where there were once only salmon. You think you're saving the fish, but what you're really doing is killing everything that feeds on that stream.

EMI EDWARDS. See, that's the thing, Professor Andrea. Maybe you're the one looking at all this wrong.

Maybe we're not animals. Maybe we're plants. And I think it's finally time to torch the Earth to see what will grow out from the ashes. Because maybe what's been growing here for way too long hasn't been flowers but weeds.

ANDREA. You'll regret this.

EMI EDWARDS. Yeah. Maybe.

So we can do this the easy way…or the fun way. You choose.

ANDREA. I choose to –

> (**ANDREA** *tries to run for it, but* **MARY** *appears on the other side of the stage and smacks her down.*)

Et Tu, Mary?

MARY. Oh shut up.

EMI EDWARDS. So, Andrea – I got a question for ya…

Who's the Shogun?

ANDREA. What?

EMI EDWARDS. Simple question. It could save you a whole lotta hurt if you answer it right.

Who's? The? Shogun?

ANDREA. …

EMI EDWARDS. Say it.

ANDREA. You are.

> **(PATRICK** *rips down the Courtyard banner!)*

TREY. All hail!

THE GEEKS. Emi Edwards!

> *(Everyone onstage, including the jocks, kneel before* **EMILY.***)*

INSIDE GIRL. And that is how the geeks inherited the Earth.

TREY. All hail!

EVERYONE. EMI EDWARDS!

> *(More students enter and kneel.)*

INSIDE GIRL. BUT –

As I told you in the beginning –

This isn't the story of how I won.

This is the story of how I fell.

TREY. All hail!

EVERYONE. EMI EDWARDS!

INSIDE GIRL. This was only the beginning to that end.

Where I needed to go next would complete my mission.

Scene Three

(Projection: Chapter Six. Samurai Sunset.)

(Projection: Five weeks later...)

EMI EDWARDS. It's been five weeks since Andrea bowed down to me.

Five weeks since all the old Shoguns had been vanquished.

EHS was now moving swimmingly for me and my geek crew.

Jillie Lee now controls the outskirts.

Patrick has Bandland.

And me and Mary stand tall where The Courtyard once stood.

None of us are getting bullied anymore.

None of us feel the oppression of our old oppressors.

We've won.

And to the winner goes the spoils.

INSIDE GIRL. Emphasis on spoiled.

(Cut to...)

*(**PATRICK** shoulder-checking **DJ MC**.)*

PATRICK. Hey! I'm sorry, buddy. I didn't mean to do that.

DJ MC. Bro, I have no interest in starting any trouble with you.

PATRICK. Dude, we're cool. Seriously. Bygones be bygones.

DJ MC. For reals?

PATRICK. Totes, man. Totes.

Oh, but PS, look at what I found on the internets.

*(**PATRICK** pulls out his phone and shows **DJ** a picture.)*

DJ MC. Yo, man, how'd you get that?

Please don't –

(**PATRICK** *hits send.*)

PATRICK. Sorry. Posted.

DJ MC. NOOOOOOOOOOO!

(*Cut to...*)

ANDREA. So what do you think?

COUNSELOR THERESA. I don't know – have you thought about – maybe – wearing less make-up? You look like a circus clown? And who dressed you today? Miley Cyrus? You look like one of George Clooney's future girlfriends.

ANDREA. What?

COUNSELOR THERESA. I'm sorry. I don't mean that. It's just...have you seen what Emily Edwards is wearing these days? That girl is looking cute. She's like Katy Perry meets Beyonce. It's refreshing.

ANDREA. I'm not here to talk fashion.

COUNSELOR THERESA. Then why are you here?

ANDREA. I want to graduate early. I'm ahead on all my credits and –

COUNSELOR THERESA. Andrea. You're a senior. You should enjoy your senior year. Why are you being so whiney?

ANDREA. I'm not being whiney. It's just...everything sucks now.

I can't walk the halls without worrying about bumping into one of those geeks –

I hear them constantly talking smack behind my back –

And when it's not behind my back it's plastered across my Instragram feed or my Tumblr –

And to top it off, I got kicked off the cheerleading squad.

COUNSELOR THERESA. That had nothing to with your peers. You weren't meeting the academic minimum to be on that squad.

ANDREA. Since when did you have to have a 4.0 GPA to cheerlead?

COUNSELOR THERESA. It's Emi's idea. Really smart, right?

She's like "Cheerleaders should be celebrated for their brains, not by how short their skirts are." So true. I love her!

ANDREA. You love Emi Edwards?

COUNSELOR THERESA. I've always loved Emi Edward.

ANDREA. I hate this so hard.

COUNSELOR THERESA. Listen, Andrea, High School only lasts for a moment. Trust me, you'll miss it when its gone...

Or you'll get hired as a guidance counselor four years later and come back to listen to all you brats, whatever.

What I'm saying is, you're going to be fine.

"It gets better."

ANDREA. I just want to go home...

INSIDE GIRL. The power dynamic had totally shifted.

I thought I was making a difference. But looking at what was happening all around, as the old saying goes, power corrupts. Absolute power corrupts –

EMI EDWARDS. OH. SHUT. UP!

INSIDE GIRL. What?

EMI EDWARDS. What you should be saying is –

YAY, WE WON!

GO US!

THE END!

INSIDE GIRL. I'm not going to say that.

EMI EDWARDS. I saved the school. That's all that anyone needs to know.

INSIDE GIRL. This is saving the school?

EMI EDWARDS. It's part of my plan.

INSIDE GIRL. What plan is that?

EMI EDWARDS. One focus –

One goal –

One objective –

No more Shoguns.

INSIDE GIRL. Then what are you? What are we?

EMI EDWARDS. We're making a difference.

INSIDE GIRL. Just 'cause you're now the ones bullying instead of the ones getting bullied doesn't make this right. Seriously, is this what this was all for? A revenge plot? You crush the Royals.

Patrick gets to be the one doing the pushing instead of the one being pushed. What about Laura? What does she get?

EMI EDWARDS. Laura?

INSIDE GIRL. You do remember Laura, right?

The first girl you saved. The girl this all started for. What about her?

EMI EDWARDS. Right. Laura.

INSIDE GIRL. Can't remember her, can you?

EMI EDWARDS. Trust me I haven't forgotten about her. She's the one I'm saving – the one I'm saving for last.

INSIDE GIRL. What's that supposed to mean?

EMI EDWARDS. What do you think I mean?

INSIDE GIRL. What? You're not going to fight her as well, right?

EMI EDWARDS. Well, if I really want to pull it off – to get the school to be scared of me.

To really be terrorized by me.

It's not enough that I took out all the old A-listers.

I gotta take out those who peeps think I care about.

INSIDE GIRL. Are you insane?

You can't do this.

I won't let you!

      *(**INSIDE GIRL** attacks **EMI**.)*

      *(But **EMI** knocks her on her ass.)*

EMI EDWARDS. This isn't Fight Club, Tyler Durden. We don't share this body.

You're my conscience, I'm the one who gets to choose who we punch.

This is my story. You're just here to tell it. So tell it.

INSIDE GIRL. No. More. Shoguns.

(Cut to…)

(TREY *and* **LAURA** *eating lunch.)*

LAURA. I can't believe you eat so much.

TREY. I can't believe you eat kale. Is that even considered food?

(He tries it.)

(He spits it out.)

Mmm. That's delicious.

LAURA. Oh shut it.

(They share a kiss.)

(EMI *strolls up and knocks their food out of their hands.)*

TREY. Hey! What are you –

EMI EDWARDS. Sit. Down.

TREY. Yes, ma'am.

LAURA. Hey Emi. How are you?

EMI EDWARDS. You and me. After school. In the field.

LAURA. What?

EMI EDWARDS. You heard me.

LAURA. Why?

EMI EDWARDS. I just don't like you.

LAURA. You want to beat me up?

EMI EDWARDS. No, I want to fight you. But if you just wanna stand there and let me smack the crap out of you, that'll work too. Either way, the result's gonna be the same.

TREY. You can't. She hasn't done anything to you.

EMI EDWARDS. Oh shut up, Captain America. Don't think I haven't forgotten that you tried to attack me yourself and if it weren't for your ex-girlfriend, you would have beat me up without a second thought.

LAURA. That's not true. He wouldn't –

EMI EDWARDS. He wouldn't what?

LAURA. Attack you.

EMI EDWARDS. Oh really? Is that what you think?

Trey.

Tell her.

TREY. It's true.

LAURA. What?

EMI EDWARDS. Yeah, he's not a good guy. But whatevs – neither am I.

So. You and me after school?

LAURA. No.

EMI EDWARDS. What was that?

LAURA. I said no. I won't fight you.

EMI EDWARDS. Fine. Have it your way. I guess I'll just have to post more nude-y pics of you later.

TREY. What?

EMI EDWARDS. Oh. You didn't think Andrea had the computer skills to hack into your Dropbox, did you?

No, that was me, stupid.

You're welcome?

TREY. You did that?

LAURA. Why are you saying this?

TREY. Why did you do it?

EMI EDWARDS. Maybe I wanted to make sure I stayed invisible.

Maybe if everyone's focus was on you, maybe it wouldn't have been on me.

Or maybe I regretted saving your giant fat ass and just wanted to see your big ol' butt squirm.

Either way, you fight me. Or you're going down in more ways than one.

TREY. No, I'm not going to let you –

*(**EMI** strikes **TREY** in the throat.)*

EMI EDWARDS. Also I'll beat up your boyfriend. What do you say?

LAURA. See you after school.

EMI EDWARDS. Cool.

Have a good lunch!

(Cut to…)

INSIDE GIRL. You think you know yourself. You think you have a clue about what makes you click.

But it's not until you really get pushed that you really get to see what kind of person you really are. And that's not always pretty.

*(**MARY** gets in **EMI**'s face.)*

MARY. Hey!

EMI EDWARDS. What are you doing here?

MARY. Did you challenge Laura Austin to a fight?

EMI EDWARDS. Uh. Maybe.

MARY. Why?

EMI EDWARDS. I have my reasons.

MARY. What reasons?

EMI EDWARDS. Don't worry about it.

MARY. Don't walk away from me. What's wrong with you?

EMI EDWARDS. Nothing. I just – I just need to do this, okay? You won't understand.

MARY. I understand that you're going to go one-on-one with a girl who has no chance at beating you. I've seen you fight. It'll be like a kid trying to box a grown man. This is not fair.

When were you going to tell me about this, huh?

EMI EDWARDS. I wasn't.

MARY. You weren't.

EMI EDWARDS. No, you weren't supposed to know –

MARY. How am I not going to know about this? Everyone in the school –

EMI EDWARDS. You said you had a Beta Club trip.

MARY. I'm not going to go on it now.

EMI EDWARDS. Just trust me, okay?

MARY. That's the problem. I keep trusting you. And you keep breaking my heart.

EMI EDWARDS. Listen. This is my last fight. I swear. No more duels after today.

MARY. You just need to get your rocks off one last time, is that it?

EMI EDWARDS. It's not that simple.

MARY. Sure it is.

I'll make it simple. Don't do it.

Let go of this fight. For me. Mary. Your bestfriend. Your girlfriend.

I'm asking you to stop.

What do you say?

(*Beat.*)

EMI EDWARDS. I can't. I have to.

MARY. I should have known. It's always about Emi. Even after all these years, you still won't listen to me. It's just about you and about what you want.

EMI EDWARDS. This time it is about us.

MARY. Screw you.

Don't do that.

Have fun doing whatever you have to do.

But you don't have to do it with me anymore.

I'm done.

EMI EDWARDS. Please no. Please.

MARY. For the record, I hope Laura beats the crap out of you.

INSIDE GIRL. It was all part of a plan. I just didn't know if I had the heart to go through with it now.

But she was gone, the school hated me, I'm even ignoring my own common sense to do this...

So what has to be done –

Will be done.

> *(Cut to...)*

> *(Projection: The Last Fight.)*

> *(Spotlight on* **EMI** *and on* **LAURA**.*)*

There's five things you need to know about this upcoming battle.

One – there's absolutely no way that Laura has a chance in the world at beating me.

I mean – look at her – she has zero skills.

Zero athletic ability.

This is no Shogun, this is a girl who dots her i's with hearts.

LAURA. It's true. I totally do that.

INSIDE GIRL. Two – I chose the field because there's plenty of room out here for the entire school to come out and witness my grand moment.

Three – I sorta kinda might have been lying about posting those pics.

> *(Cut to...)*

TREY. What do you mean "she's lying?"

LAURA. I know she didn't post them.

TREY. So it WAS Andrea?

LAURA. No.

TREY. Then who?

LAURA. Me.

TREY. What?

LAURA. I did it.

You wouldn't understand. It was just that – I didn't want to be invisible anymore. Maybe it wasn't the right move. Maybe it was totally stupid. But I knew perfectly well what I was putting out there. I actually thought they were all good shots of me. I though I looked pretty in them.

TREY. That's crazy.

LAURA. You have no idea, Trey…

Everyone sees you.

You walk in a room and you radiate.

You're beautiful.

I'm just – I'm just some girl.

TREY. Hey.

That's not true.

I see you.

I see you and I think you're beautiful.

Gorgeous.

The prettiest girl I've ever kissed.

Listen to me, I love you.

LAURA. You do?

TREY. I do.

And you're right – those shots of you were hot.

(*They kiss.*)

But then why does Emi want to fight you?

LAURA. I don't know. But I know why I want to fight her now.

TREY. Why?

LAURA. Simple.

No one hits my boyfriend.

INSIDE GIRL. Four – Yes, though this is totally manipulative. And not how I would recommend anyone treat their lovers. But, yeah, I totally knew Mary was going to find out about this fight.

EMI EDWARDS. Hey DJ!

DJ MC. Yes, man.

EMI EDWARDS. I need to put some gossip in the whisper chain. I need everyone to know about me and Laura's fight. Can you broadcast that for me?

DJ MC. Of course I can.

If you want a rumor spread, we'll just text your bestie and make it look like a secret.

EMI EDWARDS. My bestie?

(**DJ** *pulls out his phone and starts a new text.*)

DJ MC. Hey Andrea. Don't tell anyone. But Emi Edwards is gonna fight Laura this afternoon.

Crazy, right? I think she's gone insane. Send.

INSIDE GIRL. And five – I'm scared out of my mind right now because this is indeed my last fight. And what I gotta pull off is something I've never had to do before. I have to fight my instincts.

I have to learn how to go against all my natural proclivities.

I have to stop being me which is really really hard.

Because Five – I'm throwing this fight.

No. More. Shoguns.

(*A badass drum beat.*)

(*Slowly, a spotlight up on* **EMI EDWARDS**, *a geekster girl.*)

(*There's blood on her fists and lips.*)

They will fear us.

They will respect us.

They will cower.

> *(Lights up on* LAURA.*)*

> *(Equally geeky, equally bloody, equally pissed off.)*

But to get there, we will have to become as cold-blooded and single-minded as those who terrorized us.

> *(*EMI *and* LAURA *face each other.)*

For us to win, we will fight.

> *(The drums begin to become more rapid and violent in tempo.)*

> *(*BIG LAURA *slugs* EMI *in the face.)*

> *(*EMI *hits the ground hard.)*

> *(And in the greatest fight ever to bee seen on any theatrical stage ever,* EMI *and* LAURA *fight.)*

> *(However* INSIDE GIRL *is also part of this fight and manipulates it so* LAURA *can block all of* EMI*'s hits and so* EMI *takes every shot* LAURA *sends at her.)*

MARY. What's happening? She's not fighting back.

Stop!

STOP!

> *(*LAURA *pounces and begins laying in kicks and punches onto* EMI*'s torso and face.)*

> *(*EMI *tries to fight back, but it's futile.)*

> *(Lights come up on the rest of the school who are all cheering for* LAURA.*)*

> *(*LAURA *picks up the beaten* EMI *who smiles back a bloody smile.)*

INSIDE GIRL. What they don't know is we have them exactly where we want them.

> *(*LAURA *hits* EMI *in the mouth.)*

MARY. Don't!

> (**LAURA** *shoves* **EMI** *to the ground and punches her some more as the crowd envelops them.*)

No! Get away! Get away from her!

> (*They finally disperse and* **EMI** *is on the ground, beaten.*)

LAURA. I'm so sorry.

MARY. Go away.

Emi. Em. I'm right here. I'm right here, baby. I got you. I got you.

> (**MARY** *lifts* **EMI** *limp body to her own.*)

INSIDE GIRL. A samurai is singular in their vision.

A single focus.

Sometimes to win the battle, you win by using your mind, not your fists.

To defeat a superior swordsman, Miyamoto Musashi had to trick The Demon Sasaki Kojiro into staring into the sun.

For me to save my school, I had to become that sun everyone was staring into. I had to blind them from who I really was – to make them believe I was the real bad guy in this story.

But in fact, I'm not a baddie.

Or a samurai.

Or a ronin.

I'm just a girl who longs to hang with her bestie on the daily. That's all.

> (*Cut to…*)

> (**MARY** *mending* **EMI**'s *wounds.*)

> (**EMI** *slowly wakes up.*)

MARY. Hey! Hey. How are you doing?

EMI EDWARDS. I've definitely had better days than this.

MARY. Why didn't you tell me?

EMI EDWARDS. Tell you what?

MARY. That you were going to throw that fight.

EMI EDWARDS. Would you have let me do it if I did?

MARY. No.

EMI EDWARDS. That's why.

MARY. Why'd you do it?

EMI EDWARDS. Maybe because I wanted to save the kingdom.

Maybe I wanted to go back to being invisible.

Or maybe...

I just wanted to make out with the princess some more.

> (**MARY** *goes to kiss* **EMI.**)

> *(It hurts.)*

OW! OR NOT! Busted lips. That hurts like crazy.

MARY. Sorry!

EMI EDWARDS. How about you just hold me?

MARY. "As you wish."

> *(They hug.)*

> *(The girls end up slow-dancing to music like "I Never Dreamed" by The Cookies.*)*

> *(Lights down.)*

End of Play

---

*A license to produce *Begets* does not include a performance license for "I Never Dreamed." The publisher and author suggest that the licensee contact ASCAP or BMI to ascertain the rights holder to acquire permission for performance of this song. If permission is unattainable, the licensee should create an original composition in a similar style. For further information, please see music use note on page 3.